Funeral Urn

"That girl," she said, "Bess Tuckett. How did she die?"

The man shook his head. "I'm afraid I don't know. Bit before my time, and I'm a newcomer here. A mere twenty years." He peered at the urn. "Rather good work, isn't it? More skillful than the usual village masonry."

"And more explicit." Margot once more touched the stone. "Look at the plants he's chosen. Foxglove, oleander, tobacco, saffron and yew, moonflower, hemlock and belladonna. Every one of the plants in that urn produces a deadly poison. They make a strange epitaph, don't you think, for a nineteen-year-old girl?"

Other titles in the Walker British Mystery Series

Peter Alding • MURDER IS SUSPECTED
Peter Alding • RANSOM TOWN
Jeffrey Ashford • SLOW DOWN THE WORLD
Jeffrey Ashford • THREE LAYERS OF GUILT
Pierre Audemars • NOW DEAD IS ANY MAN
Marion Babson • DANGEROUS TO KNOW
Marion Babson • THE LORD MAYOR OF DEATH
Brian Ball • MONTENEGRIN GOLD
Josephine Bell • A QUESTION OF INHERITANCE
Josephine Bell • TREACHERY IN TYPE
Josephine Bell • VICTIM
W. J. Burley • DEATH IN WILLOW PATTERN
W. J. Burley • TO KILL A CAT
Desmond Cory • THE NIGHT HAWK
Desmond Cory • UNDERTOW
John Creasey • THE BARON AND THE UNFINISHED PORTRAIT
John Creasey • HELP FROM THE BARON
John Creasey • THE TOFF AND THE FALLEN ANGELS
John Creasey • TRAP THE BARON
June Drummond • FUNERAL URN
June Drummond • SLOWLY THE POISON
William Haggard • THE NOTCH ON THE KNIFE
William Haggard • THE POISON PEOPLE
William Haggard • TOO MANY ENEMIES
William Haggard • VISA TO LIMBO
William Haggard • YESTERDAY'S ENEMY
Simon Harvester • MOSCOW ROAD
Simon Harvester • ZION ROAD
J. G. Jeffreys • SUICIDE MOST FOUL
J. G. Jeffreys • A WICKED WAY TO DIE
J. G. Jeffreys • THE WILFUL LADY
Elizabeth Lemarchand • CHANGE FOR THE WORSE
Elizabeth Lemarchand • STEP IN THE DARK
Elizabeth Lemarchand • SUDDENLY WHILE GARDENING
Elizabeth Lemarchand • UNHAPPY RETURNS
Laurie Mantell • A MURDER OR THREE
John Sladek • BLACK AURA
John Sladek • INVISIBLE GREEN

JUNE DRUMMOND
Funeral Urn

WALKER AND COMPANY · NEW YORK

First published in the United States of America
in 1977 by the Walker Publishing Company, Inc.

This paperback edition first published in 1984.

ISBN: 0-8027-3048-5

Library of Congress Catalog Card Number: 76-57858

Printed in the United States of America

10 9 8 7 6 5 4 3 2 1

AUTHOR'S NOTE

Most tales spring from one central idea. Early in 1975, such an idea occurred to me. I envisaged a tombstone in a country graveyard, and on the stone the carving of a funeral urn filled with flowers and leaves—all of them poisonous.

During the next few months I was busy with other work, but in May I started to construct this present book. There evolved the imaginary Suffolk village of East Amber, and its vicar Coker Brown.

When the manuscript was half-completed, I chanced to pull from my bookshelf my old copy of T. S. Eliot's "East Coker", which I had not opened for many years. I re-read it then and there, and was struck by the fact that many of its lines could serve as chapter headings for my book, so apt they were—proof perhaps of how fine poetry is absorbed and retained beyond the level of conscious thought.

*　　*　　*

Home is where one starts from. As we grow older
The world becomes stranger, the pattern more
   complicated
Of dead and living. Not the intense moment
Isolated, with no before and after,

But a lifetime burning in every moment
And not the lifetime of one man only
But of old stones that cannot be deciphered.
There is a time for the evening under starlight,
A time for the evening under lamplight
(The evening with the photograph album).
Love is most nearly itself
When here and now cease to matter.
Old men ought to be explorers
Here or there does not matter
We must be still and still moving
Into another intensity
For a further union, a deeper communion
Through the dark cold and the empty desolation,
The wave cry, the wind cry, the vast waters
Of the petrel and the porpoise. In my end is my
   beginning.

from "East Coker", by T. S. Eliot

I

THE PETROL GAUGE registered empty.

Already the engine of the Fiat had begun to falter, but its driver seemed indifferent to the fact. There was something flaccid and careless in the way she sat, hands loose on the wheel.

Ahead of her a tractor was chugging up the last slope towards the saddle, its bulk filling the left-hand track. She made no attempt to slacken pace, but let the car lurch forward to overtake just before the blind crest. The tractor man's head jerked round. He shouted and swerved. The Fiat cut in ahead of him.

On the far side of the rise, the road did not zig-zag, but dropped in a long sharp line towards a valley wide and flat, sombre and secretive in that autumn dusk, crossed by a tumbling river and threaded by mist that hurried inland from the east. There was a village some three miles to the right—or was it closer? The haze made it appear to shift, its church tower awash among floating trees, its buildings now visible, now lost to sight. On the left, in open fields, stood a great house, its many windows dark.

The Fiat stuttered and died. The woman let impetus carry it onward, slowly at first and then faster and faster to breakneck speed. A copse whirled past, a field of wheat. The land flattened. Out of the gloom sprang a wide grass verge, more trees, and a stone bridge. The sound of the river beat on the air.

Slower. Slower. The woman dragged at the steering wheel and the car slewed right, coming to rest on the stretch of grass, with its bonnet a few inches from a dry-stone wall.

It was very quiet. Puffs of mist billowed past the windows. The woman closed her eyes and leaned her head back. Presently she heard, on the hill behind her, the drumming of the tractor's engine.

II

"WHAT IN HELL do you think you're doing?"

He was yelling as he climbed down from the perch seat; a sinewy young man in denim overalls. He clumped across the turf to the car, leaned down and glared at her. "You are driving like a lunatic!"

A lot of answers went through her mind. I am a lunatic, I don't give a damn what happens, mind your own bloody business. In the end she said nothing. He bent forward and sniffed. She turned her face petulantly aside.

"Okay, so you're sober." He glanced at the petrol gauge. "Also clear out of gas, and sense." He withdrew his head, marched round the car, opened the passenger door and climbed in. Leaning an elbow on the back of the seat, he watched her. "Where are you bound for?"

He had an extraordinary appearance, she thought. The cheek-bones were very pronounced, the mouth full and the eyes sharply slanted. She had seen the features before. Or was that an illusion? She had many illusions. His hair was docked in a pudding-bowl cut. Rural Suffolk? The voice was wrong. Overtones of Harlem, Merseyside . . . odd.

"Come on." His fingers began an impatient tattoo. "Where are you for, lady?"

"As far as possible." She was too tired to argue with

him or anyone else. She considered him with bright hatred, willing him to go away.

"Run till you drop?" He shook his head. "Well, this is East Amber, and the fog'll keep you here tonight. Leave the wheels and I'll walk you to The Ram. Over the bridge. Not far."

He climbed out, beckoning her to do the same. After a moment she complied. It was the best way to be rid of him. She had learned in hospital that argument attracted attention. She started to walk.

"Where's your bag?" he said.

"What?"

"Suitcase, clobber? Umh?"

She went back and tried to lug her case from the back seat. He took it from her. She realised that she was shivering with cold. The trees huddled along both sides of the road dripped damp, the sedges lay flat in the brimming current. As they trod across the bridge, their steps made little sound.

It was in midstream that the fear caught her, a wave of fear that seemed to be born not of herself but somehow of her surroundings. Suffocating. She checked so suddenly that her companion trod on her heel.

"Now what?"

"This place. There's something..." She could hardly speak. She stared wildly about at the silent woods and rushing water. "It's wrong. Isn't it? I feel..."

He made no answer but gripped her by the upper arm and hurried her on, over the bridge and down a short length of road, to where a building loomed. Light streamed from the open door on to muddy cobblestones. Overhead swung the gilded sign of The Ram.

III

THE INN WAS Jacobean, and very large. An oaken
counter sailed like a galleon above black and white tiles,
and at the back of the hall the carved figures of Adam and
Eve supported an elaborate mantel. The fire was not yet
lit.

"For the night, is it?" The middle-aged woman behind
the desk swung the guest-book round. "You'll be wanting
a lock-up garage, will you?"

"Car's stuck, my dearie-o," interpolated the young man,
and leaned forward to tap the open page of the book. "Sign
here, girl. Got a name, have you?"

"Wootten."

"Go on then, write it."

She wrote Margot Wootten while he watched her. She
was afraid that he meant to introduce himself, but he stood
back, while the receptionist spoke her piece about tea or
coffee in the morning and breakfast seven thirty to nine.

She should ask his name. That would be common
courtesy, but it proved to be beyond her. She did manage
to mumble thanks for his help.

He smiled without rancour. "No trouble. I'll tell Will
Asher at the garage to fill the tank for you. Is it locked?
Better gimme the key, I'll fix it for you. Sleep well." And
he turned and left her.

11

A small girl showed Margot her room. It was languorously warm and smelled of camphor-wood. Margot undressed and took a bath. She rummaged through her case, found her pills, shook one out and put the bottle away. She sat for a while looking at the pill on the palm of her hand. She hated taking the things, but Seuffert had been insistent. Said too many people took too many pills, but she didn't take enough. More of everything, he had told her, more food and sleep and medication. Don't wear the hair-shirt, they have gone out of fashion.

She climbed into bed and put out the light. A faint gleam shone through the window from outside. It showed her the telephone on the bedside table. She picked up the receiver and a voice said "Switchboard".

"Can you get me the Birmingham General Hospital? Maternity department?"

But waiting, she lost her courage. She heard the operator say, "I have a call for you from Mrs Wootten. East Amber," and another voice a long way off made some reply, and then she hung up. She lay still, imagining the conversation she might have had:

"Can you tell me if Mrs Patrick Wootten has been admitted?"

"Who is it calling?"

"This is Mrs Patrick Wootten."

"I'm afraid I don't understand . . ."

"It's quite simple. This is Mrs Patrick Wootten, the genuine, famous, barren Mrs Wootten, calling from East Amber to wish you all in hell."

She swung over in the bed and smashed her fist hard into the pillow. The bell beside her pealed twice and she ignored it. She lay for some time while resentment and jealousy conjured image after image before her, but at length the sleeping pill took effect.

12

IV

THE FIRST THING she heard when she woke next morning was the sound of the river. She got out of bed and went to the window. The course ran close to the back of the inn, narrow but turbulent. Downstream, it seemed to widen into a ford, but even there it looked dangerous.

There must have been heavy rain in the night. The ground was still sodden and the sky surly.

She went down to breakfast thinking that she would leave straight afterwards, and drive to the coast. Perhaps she might cross to France. They wouldn't pursue her there.

But in the event the idea came to nothing. While she was drinking her coffee, she was called from the dining-room to speak to the garage proprietor, Will Asher.

"I took a look at your car, Mrs Wootten. Needs a lot of work."

"It'll have to wait."

"Can't wait. You've bin hammerin' that engine, drivin' 'thout oil er water. Overheatin' and yer brakes are up to maggots. I'd need her for today at least."

"Impossible. I intend to leave this morning."

Asher gave a snort of contempt. "Right, you do that. Drive off, kill yerself an' a couple more into the bargain. I heard the way you drove into Amber. Criminal, that is."

Her old betrayer, the puling honesty that had lost her

so much, kept her from hitting back at him. Asher persisted.

"Do the work, will I?"

"I suppose so."

"I'll give you a quote before I get stuck in."

So there she was, marooned in this god-damn backwater.

At half past nine she went out to buy something to read. The Ram, she found, stood at the junction of three roads. One led back across the bridge. One veered round the side of the inn, past a school-house and some cottages, to what looked like a new housing estate. The third led to the village proper.

Margot took this road.

She realised almost at once that East Amber was one of those shrunken towns that in the seventeenth and eighteenth centuries prospered from the wool trade, but then dwindled and were forgotten by the world.

The dominant building was the church, enormous, planted upon a round knoll and crowned by a massive tower. On one side of it lay its graveyard, and on the other a row of shops. Opposite this display of lay and secular power was a large market-place, with buildings on three sides. Quarried stone, all from the same source, but the flanking wings more recent than the central one. The old Guild-hall, perhaps, with Victorian additions?

She walked slowly on.

A police station, a supermarket, a post office, and a solid phalanx of cottages, with good walls and gardens. There was half-timbering, some brick and stone. Amber had been beautiful once.

When the houses began to thin out, she turned back, stopped at the supermarket and bought a paperback of *The Gulag Archipelago*. The main street seemed busier now. Was Wednesday shopping day?

She found herself back at the church. "St Ringan's"

14

said the lettering on the board at the gate. What was the old saint doing so far south? The grounds were neatly kept, but the fabric of the walls and bell tower had a look of inadequate care. Maintained to safety limits, but no more. One might shed tears about that, if one cared for religion, or architecture.

She glanced into the porch. There was a table with the usual depressing literature, untouched for months, and beyond that a damp green gloom.

She turned back and walked through a gap in yew hedges, into the graveyard. She'd visited a lot of those at the time when she forgot how to sleep. She'd looked with envy at the turf, at the quiet trees, at the mounds where pretence ended. Now, she was well enough to realise that she'd been freaking out; but she remained grateful to the dead, who asked no questions and made no accusations.

She wandered along clay walks, and by habit noticed the plants and mosses that fringed them.

She studied the headstones.

There were a lot of Hoggs in Amber. Tidbolds. Tucketts. The dates went back a long way. Some of the stones were too smooth to read.

The Tuckett tombs were grouped together in the south-west corner of the yard. Some of them were pretty grand, with pompous epitaphs, and inscriptions to people named Jeremiah or Nathaniel.

At the western end, farthest from the church, there was a stretch of sunken ground close to the hedge, and there she found the grave of Bess Tuckett.

There was nothing to distinguish it from the others. The stone bore the name, the dates 1894–1913, and above that some ornamental carving. Margot could not have told what drew her closer, made her straddle the strip of grass and peer at the carving. It represented some sort of urn, she thought, but there was a heavy layer of lichen over it.

15

She scratched at the growth, which flaked away in small sections.

Something caught her attention. She bent nearer, then leaned down and searched hastily for a twig. Using that, she soon had the carving exposed.

It was a funeral urn, delicately expressed, gracefully fluted, and filled with easily identifiable flowers, berries and leaves. She traced them with her finger-tip. Foxglove. Saffron. Oleander. . . .

A voice broke in on her. "Good morning."

She glanced up sharply. A man was coming through a wicket gate almost buried in the fence. He wore jeans, boots, a white jersey and a clerical collar. He came smiling to her side. "Cleaning up for us? I'm afraid these things are in poor condition. No money for upkeep."

Margot was too intent upon her discovery to snub his friendliness.

"That girl," she said, "Bess Tuckett. How did she die?"

The man shook his head. "I'm afraid I don't know. Bit before my time, and I'm a newcomer here. A mere twenty years." He peered at the urn. "Rather good work, isn't it? More skilful than the usual village masonry."

"And more explicit." Margot once more touched the stone. "Look at the plants he's chosen. Foxglove, oleander, tobacco, saffron and yew, moonflower, hemlock and belladonna. Every one of the plants in that urn produces a deadly poison. They make a strange epitaph, don't you think, for a nineteen-year-old girl?"

V

"IT COULD HAVE been chance." The man seemed both interested and disconcerted.

"Monumental masons," said Margot, "are pedestrian souls. They might choose a yew leaf to symbolise grief. But why saffron?"

"Star-naked Boys," mused the other. "Yes, it is odd. Tell you what, come up to the house for a cup of coffee and we'll ask my wife. She was born here. She may know something." He smiled as Margot hesitated. "Come along."

As she followed him ungraciously through the clipped grass walks, he said, "It was smart of you to recognise those plants."

"Hardly. I'm a botanist."

"Indeed? Where?"

"The Kirkwood Research Centre." She supposed that was true. Owen had insisted on keeping her job open, although she had made it clear she would not go back. He had made some clumsy quip about allowing the oak to grow its callus. She had answered that a dead oak grows no callus.

"I'm Coker Brown," the man was telling her, "vicar of St Ringan's and strolling preacher at a dozen others." He led her through another gate and a neglected garden towards a sprawling Victorian building in need of a coat of paint. On the strip of lawn before it, three boys aged about twelve were taking a bicycle to pieces and spreading the parts on a sheet of blue plastic. Mr Brown ignored them, pushed open the back door and ushered his guest straight into a large and cluttered living-room. Without noticing detail, Margot got the impression that this was the nerve-centre of a parish as well as a family. At a table against the far wall, a woman was sorting packs of old playing cards into piles. She looked up as they entered.

"Hallo. You're early." She got up from her chair. She was very tall, with a mass of tightly-curling yellow hair, a bright attentive gaze, and a gap between her front upper teeth. She smiled at Margot.

"Zillah," said her husband, "what do you know about Bess Tuckett, who died in 1913?"

"Not much." Zillah set down the bundle of cards she held. "Why do you ask?"

"We noticed something..." Coker Brown stopped short and turned to Margot. "I am so sorry. I never even learned your name."

"Margot Wootten."

"Mrs?"

"Doctor."

"Dr Wootten pointed out an odd circumstance to me. The carving on Bess Tuckett's tombstone shows an urn full of poisonous plants. Strange, eh?"

It seemed to Margot that as he spoke he directed at his wife a warning glance.

"Could we have coffee?"

"Of course."

The girl moved off, and Coker Brown pulled forward an armchair for Margot, set a table beside it, added an ashtray. He was, by his looks, about forty years old, and had one of those creased, ingenuous faces that people like on sight. As he took his place on the sofa, he said, "There's no Bess Tuckett in our parish guide-book, though there's a Tuckett on just about every page. Tucketts, Hoggs, and Campions, those are the village patronymics, right back to Plantagenet times."

He talked about local history until Zillah came back with the coffee, which she poured into pottery mugs. When they were all served, she sat down and leaned her elbows on her knees.

"Someone must have given specific orders for the tombstone," she said. "No mason would deliberately choose poisonous plants."

"That's what Dr Wootten feels."

"Well then, someone told him what to carve. But why?"

"To work off an old grudge?"

"On a dead woman? Rather small-minded! And how about libel?"

"I doubt whether one could make a libel charge stick, in such circumstances!"

"And surely, someone must have noticed the nature of those plants before today. . . ."

"One would have thought so."

"Yet no one has mentioned it."

"Perhaps the villagers of the time agreed with the view that Bess Tuckett was poisonous. More likely, they couldn't tell one plant from another. Country-folk are surprisingly ignorant about flora." Mr Brown smiled. "After all, it's not every day that we have a Doctor of Botany in Amber."

They were both looking at Margot. She saw in their eyes the watchful expression she had come to dread. They had caught the scent of trouble on her. In a moment they would close in, inquisitive, ruthless, determined to break down her defences and dig their fingers into her heart and brain.

She stumbled to her feet. "I have to go now."

"My dear, you haven't finished your coffee."

"I don't want it." Be brutally rude, that was the answer, smash your way out, take refuge in fury. "Really, I can't think why we should waste time on a woman who's been dead for half a century. It can't matter a damn." She was pleased that her voice was under control. It sounded as cold as ice and it was having effect. They were staring at her as if she might explode before their eyes. That calmed her further. She began to walk steadily to the door. But Zillah Brown got there first, blocking her path, leaning down that fuzzy gold head like a great dandelion, and saying something quite extraordinary.

"If Bess Tuckett can help you, then you mustn't brush her aside."

"I'm not interested in Bess Tuckett. . . ."

". . . She was drowned in the river, that's all I know. It's sort of an old rumour. I'll find out what I can and come and tell you."

"I don't want to hear. I'm getting out of the place as soon as I can. Now will you let me pass, please?"

Zillah stood aside and Margot sped from the house, across the lawn, down the tangled garden. It had started to drizzle. Bright sparks of moisture, burning on the wind, stung her eyes. She ran most of the way back to the inn, went straight to her room, curled up on the bed and lay absolutely still. In the past, she'd usually been able to mend her cocoon that way, but today it didn't work. The protective threads would not knit, and she lay exposed to the world. Like Bess Tuckett.

At twelve she telephoned Will Asher and asked when she might have the car.

He grunted dourly. "Gotta re-line the brakes. Lucky if she's ready tomorrow."

She didn't waste effort arguing. She had to have the car, it was her only means of escape.

The sound of the river was very loud. She went to the window and looked out. The level of the water had risen in the past few hours. The ford was many feet wider, turbulent with brown foam.

A woman in long skirts would easily lose her footing there, and be swept downstream.

She turned away abruptly; went to the bathroom, washed, came back to sit at the dressing-table.

It was strange. One looked in a mirror and saw this person making herself tidy, combing back her short brown hair, tidying her mouth into a firm downward line, tidying her eyes to a smooth, blank grey. One recognised this person but one did not want to associate with her, one did not like her. She was gullible and careless and above all treacherous ... like now ... leaning forward in that sly way with soft phrases. "I could stay here," she was saying, "I'm tired of running. I could give up and sleep forever."

Margot rebuked her loudly. "What use is that? You know you have to keep moving, you have to fight, or you're finished."

"They'd help you."

"Don't be a fool, you can't trust them."

"You trust them. You take their pills."

"Only for sleep, nothing else. No pain-killers, no drugs, no pity. No pity from them."

"But self-pity." The mouth smiled sideways.

"No self-pity."

"I'm frightened!"

"You're hungry, that's all. It's lunch-time. And after lunch, a walk."

The other face brightened, almost smiled. "Oh yes. A walk. September, that means sea asters, harebells, lords and ladies. It's such a long time since I saw those . . ."

Margot picked up her handbag and started for the door.

VI

SHE LEFT THE RAM just after two o'clock, and took the road through the new housing estate. It was not large. The houses had a raw look, their gardens hardly established. Margot wondered where the inhabitants worked. Ipswich, perhaps, or Kersey. There were very few of them about.

Beyond the estate, she was soon in farmland, gently undulating except for the hump of Cobbledick Hill, and obscured from time to time by drifts of rain. She stepped out briskly at first, and then old habit asserted itself and she dawdled, her eyes searching the ground. It seemed free of the soot and detergent that was spreading out from the industrial areas. The undergrowth in the ditches was flourishing.

She thought of her three years in the Amazon basin. As the new road was pushed forward, the team had worked ahead of it, struggling to record an incredible variety of plants. One had the desperate feeling that one must miss nothing. The strip of earth torn up by the bulldozers could end an entire cycle of life. There were so few people who understood that. Patrick had been sent home early to address the Ecological Conference, but how many laymen listened to words? They would listen, soon, to hunger. When the endangered species was man. . . .

She was passing a small copse. A pheasant clattered in the brushwood. She bent down to study the shrivelled stalks of foxglove, the dried country flowers, Herb Robert and Century. She picked a leaf of the last and bit it gently. It was well named earthgall. They took it, once, against chills and fevers.

So many plants had medicinal uses. Foxglove was poisonous, but its digitalis was a life-saver in the proper dosage. Saffron—what that ox of a vicar had called star-naked Boys—was the source of the drug that relieved gout. Poison was a matter of degree, and a poisoner must be guilty of malicious intent. Was that tombstone merely a tribute to the woman's knowledge of herbs?

On the other hand, saffron wasn't a native of Suffolk, so much as of the western sea-borders. It was odd to find it on a gravestone in East Amber.

Her thoughts being full of the Tuckett name, it startled her to see it again, this time on a freshly-painted sign-board. Tuckett's Farm. The white finger pointed along a narrow lane between high banks. She followed it, mud squelching over her shoes. She climbed a slope and emerged on its crest just as the rain lifted a little. Away to her right was the Amber river, and on her left, in a hollow of ground, stood a farmhouse with its outhouses and stables about it, and a scythe of trees behind.

Margot walked towards it. As she came nearer she could see that the house was in two parts, a central section of rough stone, and a more recent wing of cut stone. The newer wing was not without elegance, having Georgian doors and fanlights and a good slate roof.

It seemed the story of a family's prosperity. Going up in the world as the demand for woollen goods swelled. She saw that the surrounding land was still being farmed, well farmed by the look of the soil and the heavy crops.

She wondered who lived here. The young man on the tractor? Was it still a Tuckett who owned the place?

She was close enough, now, to perceive detail; the windows of the house were closed but polished, the lawn before it fairly newly clipped. Perhaps the owners were away on holiday? But surely there must be someone in charge, there'd be animals to care for? She took the muddy track that circled an orchard and emerged on the far side of the sickle of trees. This enclosed a series of buildings, a dairy and buttery, barns, stables, and three or four cottages. A man and two lads were busy milking a large number of black and white cows, and a child with lint-coloured hair was pouring swill into troughs for the pigs. Margot stood in the shelter of the trees and watched. It was only after some ten minutes that she realised she in her turn was being observed from the doorway of the nearest cottage.

The confronter was a small man in jeans, jersey and leather apron, and he presented a strange appearance, being so bent as to be almost a hunchback. His head hung forward, his mouth was slack around large and irregular teeth, and his eyes were obscured by a green shade such as one associates with printers in old films. In one hand he held a knife, with a curved blade that gleamed in the uncertain light.

"I'm sorry." Margot made an apologetic gesture. "I lost my way. Is this Tuckett's Farm?"

The little man nodded, but said nothing.

"Can you tell me how to get back to the village?"

Still he stared at her without speaking. She wondered if he might be deaf, and moved closer to him. "Amber. Can you tell me how to get back to Amber?"

For answer, he leaned back into the cottage and shouted "Win!" The call brought to his side a woman even smaller than he, though more comely. She was very fat, and wore a dress of emerald green wool, a leather apron similar to the man's and a knitted band that kept straggling white hair from her brows. The two of them looked for all the world like gnomes, the tinsmiths of the Little People.

"Yes?" The woman fixed Margot with bright eyes.

"Can you direct me to Amber?"

"I can. I can. But let me move the varnish first."

She beckoned Margot into the cottage with a sharp jerk of the elbow.

It was not a living-place, Margot saw, but a workshop. What must once have been four rooms had been knocked into one, separated only by archways. At the back was an enormous Esse stove, on which a number of singularly evil-smelling pots bubbled and steamed. In the centre of the floor was a modern steel work bench, lit by strip lighting, and strewn with an amazing clutter of knives and awls, clamps and braces, pieces of wood and ivory, paints and brushes of every kind.

But it was the walls of the room that fascinated Margot, for they were hung with musical instruments old and new; as if four centuries of long-dead musicians had hung them there, on the way through to some loftier Valhalla.

The woman, ignoring her guest, hurried straight to the stove, and rising on tip-toe shifted a large copper pot from a front plate to the back. The man resumed his place on a stool at the bench, and picked up what looked like a giant wooden pear, sliced in half along its length.

"What is it? A mandolin?"

"Mandola. About three hundred and forty year old. Been repaired before, see? No good now, the wood's gone, you couldn't play it." He had lifted off the facia board of the instrument, and his gnarled fingers touched various points inside its belly. Margot saw that the wood was

26

indeed cracked and friable, and had been patched with strips of fine gauze.

"Strappin'," affirmed the old man. "It'll hold for the purpose."

"And what is that?"

"Decor. Hang it on the wall, or sell it to America, they will. Fetch quite a nice price. We do a tidy trade."

While he was speaking, he was carefully, with a fine sable brush, painting some dark liquid over the outer edges of the gauze. That done, he dipped the brush once more into the pot, and with a quick, almost automatic skill, drew a design at the centre of the material. Margot bent closer.

"What's that?"

"Umh? Oh, that's the Amber marks. One for the Campions, one for ourselves." He lifted the piece of wood so that she could see it better. He had drawn a rudimentary coat of arms, with a campion flower at the centre; and below that, he had added a few notes of music, which she did not recognise. He caught he enquiring glance.

"Haydn," he said. "My dad used that, and his before him."

"Do you repair instruments for performance too?"

"A few. Ain't much call for that, hereabouts."

"But there was, once?"

"Oh aye. When the Festival was big, there was a lot of big names came to it. My dad was one of the best to doctor a fiddle. But things changed, an' we don't get much call for it now. Mostly they want stuff to hang on the wall."

There was contempt in his voice, and regret. Before she could question him further, his wife came bustling back.

"There, that's the varnish done. I'll walk to the gate and set you on your way."

Margot said goodbye to the old man and followed the woman from the building. They traversed the belt of trees and reached a five-barred gate. Beyond lay a surfaced road.

"This'll take you to the main road, that leads straight to Amber. Just bear right all the time."

Margot spoke the first words that came to her mind.

"That was Bess Tuckett's work-room, wasn't it?"

Small, shrewd eyes swung round to stare. "Never. She never worked in that cottage."

"Are you related to her?"

"I am not. Gibbon is my name, Winifred Gibbon, and my husband was from Colchester. There's no Tucketts left in Amber now."

"And no skilled instrument-makers?"

"They moved away, mostly."

"When?"

"After the Great War, so I'm told. We're not from Amber, only been here eighteen year. Dont know what went on before."

There was finality in the phrase, almost a warning. Mrs Gibbon waited for Margot to go through the gate, shut it firmly after her, and hurried away.

Margot started along the road, The sun was no more than a red chip on the baize horizon. She had been out for over two hours, and it seemed longer. She had the feeling that she had been afforded a glimpse of something forbidden. Strange that she should be picking up in East Amber the same signals of tribal tabu as in Xingu.

Was it simply the results of economic decay? She had discovered in the workshop the evidence of loss of old skills, and their replacement by the gimcrack modern liking for empty display. The whole area spoke clearly of departed glories.

Or was there something more singular in the way that Bess Tuckett's name conjured up, even among people who had never known her, an immediate hostility and fear?

Margot walked quickly, the fiery cold of evening cutting through her damp coat. The tower of St Ringan's rose higher above the fields, and soon after five o'clock she reached The Ram.

As she entered the warmth of the hall, someone rose from a chair near the desk and moved to meet her.

"You left your book at our house," said Zillah Brown. "I made it an excuse to come and talk to you. I've found out something about Bess Tuckett's tombstone."

VII

MARGOT ORDERED TEA which was brought to
them by the publican's wife, Nancy Rubidge. This was a
nervous woman, with a sad hare's face, and large clumsy
hands. She brightened at the sight of Zillah, and at once
suggested the tea be taken through to the private parlour
at the back of the inn.

"You'll be quieter there, the fire's on, and I'll bring you
some of the walnut cake."

This proved to be delicious, spiked with country cream
and fresh white nuts. Zillah spoke round a generous slice
of it.

"Did you get as far as Tuckett's Farm?"

"How did you know where I went?"

"Chilli Gold saw you walking out that way. He's the
chap who brought you here last night."

"I see." Margot found that she was far more tired than
she had realised. Her head was pounding. She drank a cup
of tea and let its sweetness sink into her, closed her eyes
and rubbed her neck.

"Don't go to sleep," warned Zillah. She was spreading
a series of tattered notes on the oak settle. After a while
she had them in order, and began her narrative.

"Coker told you, didn't he, that I've lived here all my
life? My grandfather was parson here, name of Hogg, and

he was a history nut. He hoarded everything he could lay hands on, and I've been scouring the attics. There are a lot of old parish registers and records. As far as I can tell from those, the Tucketts owned that farm you saw today, for almost a century and a half. The last owner was Bess. It came to her when her parents died, which was when she was sixteen. The parents, Joel and Ellen Tuckett, died in a typhoid epidemic that knocked off a lot of people, including visitors who'd come for the Festival."

"What Festival was that?"

"Same as always, the Amber Music Festival. It's been going for ages, on and off. At that particular time it was important. People came from all over Europe, because the Campions fixed it. The Campions were millionaires, then."

"But not now?"

"No."

"Did you find all this in the records?"

"Not the Festival bit. That's common knowledge." Zillah frowned slightly. "And I can't help being surprised that that tombstone isn't, as well. In a village, not much escapes the eye."

"Perhaps people wanted to forget Bess Tuckett."

"Perhaps."

"What happened after her parents died?"

"Another strange thing, the farm was not sold. Bess seems to have gone on living there alone. Queer, for a girl of sixteen? I suppose there must have been a man to manage the place, unless she was unusually tough and competent, and ran it herself."

"Were the Tucketts gentry?"

"No. Wealthy yeoman stock, made a lot from wool and grain, and also produced a strain of fine craftsmen. They made and repaired musical instruments. Apparently they were quite famous at one time." Zillah shuffled together

her scraps of paper. "That's all I could find in the parish records. But then I thought of the register of deaths, and searched through that. Bess was drowned at Amber ford on November 14th, 1913. It happened right at the end of the Festival fortnight."

"How?"

"I don't know. The Amber is a dangerous river, it comes down in flood very quickly because of the springs on Cobbledick Hill, and at that time the drainage system wasn't as good as it is now. Perhaps they tried to cross the ford and were caught."

"Who's they?"

"Jerome Campion of Amberside . . . that's the local Toad Hall . . . was drowned on the same day. So it's likely they were involved in the same incident."

"Were they lovers?"

"Shouldn't think so. Bess was nineteen when she died, and Jerome was forty-eight. Maybe he tried to save her."

"You'd think a story like that would have passed into local folklore."

"Unless, as you say, people wanted to wipe it from their minds. If she was a poisonous person. . . ."

Something cold touched Margot's memory. "Yesterday, when I came into Amber . . . as I crossed the bridge . . . I got the shivers." Her mouth twisted. "I've had a lot of 'em, over the past few months, but this was different. It seemed to come from outside me, from the place itself." She fixed her gaze on Zillah. "Is there a superstition about it?"

"People don't like it much. There's no story, that I know of. Haunting? You're a scientist, surely you don't believe in ghosts?"

Margot did not answer at once. "I've spent the last three years in the Amazon basin. Among primitive people, one gets to believe in the power of belief. What they have in their minds is real. It affects them, and it affects those

32

close to them. Even people who call themselves civilised have tribal patterns, they have race memories, they are influenced to an amazing degree by events they have not known. If you can call that, haunting . . . well. . . ."

"Do you think Amber ford is evil in people's mind?"

"Perhaps. If it was the scene of a tragedy, and was associated in their thoughts with fear and horror, then they might suppress the incident itself. Not speak of it. But then the fear might become superstitious. It might provoke a sort of instinctive revulsion when one passed that place."

"But you felt it, and you're not a local person."

"I was with a local man."

Zillah shrugged lightly, as if she had little time for such fancies. She gathered the papers in one hand and wagged them.

"Now I come to the interesting part. After I'd looked through the register of deaths in the Guild-hall, I went back to the attic. Grandfather kept a lot of old accounts. I found them. I checked the accounts for the funerals of Bess and Jerome. They may have been drowned on the same day, but they weren't buried on the same day, let alone at a joint service. There was rigid separation, as if the Campions wanted nothing to do with the death of Bess."

"Snobbery? The king and the beggar-maid?"

"Bess wasn't a beggar. Her farm was one of the richest in Amber. She was buried in a teak coffin with silver handles. But the stone on her grave was commissioned by the villagers. A firm in Colchester was asked to provide it. Here's the bill." Zillah held out a letter with an elaborately scrolled heading. "The stone was ordered by 'the parish of East Amber'. See? And completed 'to specification'. But there's nothing to say what that was, or who drew it up."

"Or who paid?"

33

"Perhaps they all chipped in. But then, someone must have done the collecting. And if it was a communal effort, then more than one person must have understood what that carving was meant to convey." She shook her head musingly. "Their silence, that's the puzzle."

She gathered up her papers for the last time. "I'm going to see what else I can learn. I thought I'd speak to old Ned Rubidge, that's Nancy's grandfather-in-law. He'll be at the rehearsal tonight. Why don't you come?"

"No thank you. I'm rather tired." Yet against her will Margot found herself adding, "What rehearsal?"

"Choir. Do you like music?"

"Yes." Unwillingly. "I did once."

"Then come!" Zillah got quickly to her feet. "Thank you for the tea. I'll hope to see you later. Come along to the church at half past seven. Ned and Nancy will bring you. Or if you want to hear without being seen, go up to the organ gallery. The door is on the left-hand side of the main porch, quite easy to find." And with a final gap-toothed smile, she was gone.

VIII

IT WAS BITTERLY cold in the gallery.

Margot, huddled on a wooden seat close to the rail, felt a thousand draughts sucking at her neck and ankles, and wondered what had possessed her to come.

At her back the organ pipes soared into remote shadow. Below, the choristers were gathering in the choir stalls, which looked large enough to accommodate the entire population of Amber. The church was vast, and its beauty lay in its form rather than its decor. It must have been built before the Renaissance lust for embroideries took hold. Its soaring but ponderous columns were like the first thoughts of a genius who with gaze turned inward gropes towards a half-sensed perfection.

Clearly they weren't going to use the organ tonight. There was a portable piano standing next to the organ console, and on a table near that lay an assortment of instruments; a flute, two recorders, a violin and something that could be a lute.

Margot began to be interested. Her father had been a professional musician of some note, and his special interest had been in the sixteenth- and seventeenth-century composers, particularly of choral works. He would have enjoyed tonight's backdrop.

Zillah and Coker Brown were there, and Will Asher;

and Mrs Rubidge, accompanied by an enormous old man with the fiery gaze of an ancient prophet, whom Margot took to be grandfather Ned. This colossus paid no attention to anyone, but busied himself at the miniature piano, placing a seat to his liking and sorting peevishly through a pile of music.

There were over thirty people down there now, a large choir for such a village. They were all adults, no trebles, so probably the rehearsal was secular rather than religious. No doubt they'd be terrible.

A young man came rushing up from the nave, swinging a guitar case. It was the tractor driver, not in jeans this time but in brown slacks and jersey, his hair neatly combed. What had Zillah said his name was? Gold? And a quaint first name that struck some sort of bell?

Last to arrive was an elderly exquisite with a shock of white hair, a dark green velvet smoking jacket, black pants, and leather boots. It was difficult to say whether his clothes were trendy or archaic. Was he the conductor? The others didn't like him, Margot noticed. She had worked too long with teams to miss that edgy overtone of mistrust. He had a peculiar face, the nose very long and tilted, the chin minimal, the eyes large and luminous. His taste would run to...what? Madrigals? The lesser moderns?

He was talking to Will Asher. The other choristers came down from the stalls and ranged themselves in a half moon. Soprano, alto, tenor, bass. Asher was, surprisingly, a tenor. No doubt that was what made him so arrogant, nobody liking to offend a tenor.

The Gold person was not a singer. He had taken up a position next to Mr Rubidge.

The conductor called for a chord. Old Mr Rubidge struck it. The conductor lifted his hands in a small, neat gesture, and the singing began.

It was a carol, very old, unaccompanied, in minor harmony.

> Lulla, lullay, thou little tiny child,
> I'll sing bye bye, lullay. . . .

Margot wrapped cold arms about herself. Was there to be no escape from chance? So be it, one must listen and endure. One must probe the source of pain. The thing was painful not because it was a lullaby, but because it conjured up the Madonna of Belem, a hideous effigy of pink, blue and mud-coloured wax, in the church where she had gone after Patrick's ship left. She had sat in the stuffy, dark pew, and dreamed of following him from Brazil, of reunion, conception, birth. Had she prayed? If so, she'd wasted her time.

It was ridiculous to freeze in this morgue.

She began to get to her feet, but her jacket tangled in the end of the rail and jerked her back. She fell sideways with a clatter. None of the singers glanced upward. They were absorbed in their silly tune. How foolish they looked, the croaking yokels, jaws, chests and throats in unison.

But they sang well.

Her ears admitted as much. They had discipline and musicianship. The conductor knew what he was about. He took them from the carol to another unaccompanied song, more difficult, and then spent a short while on a new work. His way of rehearsing showed he understood voices. He interrupted his singers neither too much nor too little. His instructions were clear, and showed he understood the intention of the composer.

Margot stayed where she was.

The fourth song, accompanied this time by Ned Rubidge, was a test of a different kind. "Phil the Fluter's

Ball." The choir took it skimmingly, every word and note crystalline.

They were bloody good.

At that point the conductor called a break. The choir broke ranks and moved about the chancel. Margot, hearing someone call her name, looked down to see the Browns and the tractor man below her. The Browns held each a recorder, Gold his guitar. They signalled her to come down. She shook her head. They signalled yes, come on. Reluctantly she made her way down the stairway from the gallery, back into the nave and across to the chancel. The group on the steps, holding their musical instruments and with the light shining from behind them, seemed like some old bas-relief come to life.

Zillah offered her something. It was a folio of music.

"We're going to do the Campion Cycle," she said. "Perhaps you'd like to follow the score?"

Margot took the folio. It was old and battered, and the spine had been clumsily mended at some time. Ornately emblazoned on the front cover were the words:

The Campion Cycle
Six Songs for Choir

Lyrics by Jerome Campion   Music by Randall Jecks.

She was suddenly glad she'd come. She'd heard the cycle two or three times, and always with the feeling that it was not being performed as it should be. Here, perhaps, in Campion country, she might be surprised.

She turned a page. There was a frontispiece of Jerome Campion. The engraving showed a bony face with a blond beard and an expression of restive energy.

His six lyrics were printed at the back of the folder, and

so the man's face and his words framed the music . . .
scored, Margot saw, for flute, recorder and piano.

She started up the chancel steps. Before she could settle
herself in the choir stalls, an uproar began on the chancel
floor; old Mr Rubidge and the conductor, with their faces
inches apart, bellowing their lungs out at each other.

IX

"NAW AH WON'T," roared Mr Rubidge, and danced infuriatedly for emphasis. "Ah won't play the pianner for the Cycle. Wasn't meant so and I won't do so. Lutes an' flutes an' voices is what's called for, not any piddlin' ol' pianner. So put that in yer thick nut, Mister bloody Jecks."

"Mr Rubidge." The conductor was as enraged as his critic; his prominent eyes glistened with tears of fury. "I am, after all, the composer of these songs and I believe I have a better notion than you of what is and what is not called for in the way of musical accompaniment. I arranged it for piano, flute and recorder."

"Lute, it should be," yelled Mr Rubidge. "Lute lute lute an' if yer can't see what's needed then I don't care a fish's tit for yer. Not a fish's tit."

The conductor raised both fists above his head as if he would strike Mr Rubidge down. Then he pressed the fists to his forehead and swung towards Mr Gold.

"Chilli, my dear boy. Save my sanity. Play for us."

Chilli smiled. "Can't do the piano part, Mr Jecks. But I could manage the lute part."

"There is no lute part." Jecks flung his arms wide. "Gott in Himmel there has never been a lute part. Never. Not since I wrote that score sixty-two years ago. Damn it, you know that!"

"There should be a lute part," said Chilli. "We've always wanted it."

"Your wants have nothing to do with the case!"

Chilli made no direct answer, but picked up the lute from the table at his hand, walked to the piano stool and sat down. He cradled the lute, sounded the strings gently, made a small adjustment, and began to play.

It was difficult music, on an obsolete instrument, but as the first sounds burst out, Margot laid aside her score and stared round-eyed. The choir had been a pleasant surprise, but this man was prodigious. The notes flew out like sparks of water, round, pure and strong. The chords had tremendous vigour. Chilli glanced up and made a jerk of the head at Will Asher, who came and stood beside him, and in a moment took up the tenor part of the first song.

The Campion lyrics formed a love cycle, as Margot knew, and the first air spoke of the lovers' encounter in the early morning by the river. There was in both words and music a sense of mystery, of passion, and of impending loss. Will's voice was no more than good, but he sang the song as if it had been written for him.

"That's it," said Margot, unaware that she spoke aloud. "That's it, that's dead right."

" 'Course it is," said Mr Rubidge, sliding into the seat next to hers. She noticed that he smelled of whisky. He leaned back and stretched out his legs. "Go on, you stupid wethers, form up around 'em."

The choir needed no telling. They were already in a half circle round Asher, song-folders in hand. At the end of the solo introduction, the chorus came in with a joyous crash. The lyricism of the first bars vanished in music that was at times tumultuous, at times only a wisp of sound, but that conveyed an exultant sense of discovery and delight. That faded, leaving two voices only, tenor and soprano, floating like thistledown in a blue sky.

41

Those too vanished. The lute continued alone, very softly, and at last was lost.

"I will not have it!" Jecks had shifted to stand behind Chilli Gold, no doubt thinking in this way to attract the choir's attention. They did not spare him a glance. He had literally to push his way into their midst. "I will not have it. The music will be performed as I wrote it, or not at all."

Will Asher showed large yellow teeth in a grin. "Won't get us to listen tonight, Mr Jecks. Not so long as Chilli's game. Best leave it over till tomorrow."

"I shall not be here tomorrow." Jecks whipped round like a little lizard. "There is such a thing as performing right, you know. And contracts. You will learn the hard way."

Jecks stormed off towards the nave. Coker Brown, as if suddenly remembering his role of peacemaker, hurried after him, but the rest of the choir was already turning its attention to the second lyric. They were, Margot guessed, set to sing for hours.

Beside her, Ned Rubidge had given way to wheezing chuckles. Margot studied him.

"You and the Gold man fixed it between you, didn't you?"

"Us an' Will did. Well, you can see 'at's how it should be. Lute, not pianner."

"It's only chance that you can pull it off . . . because Gold is an exceptional musician, and lives here in Amber."

"So he is an' so he does, an' any silly bugger could see how to use 'is talents, but that toadstool of a Jecks."

The sound of recorders and lute in unison came to their ears. The Browns and Chilli were grouped together, the vicar having apparently abandoned Jecks to his fate.

Thoughts had begun to coalesce in Margot's mind. She picked up the Campion Cycle score. Hadn't the old boy

42

said something about "sixty-two years ago?" She leaned over and touched Ned's arm.

"This Jerome Campion," she pointed at the cover of the folder, "the one who wrote the words, is that the same man as drowned in the Amber ford?"

Rubidge stopped chuckling. His eyes flickered towards her and away again.

" 'At's right."

"Was he drowned with Bess Tuckett?"

Rubidge was staring at the choir and seemed not to hear her. Margot leaned towards him.

"Was he drowned at the same time as Bess Tuckett?"

This earned a mere shake of the fingers, dismissive.

"Did you know Bess?" demanded Margot.

At her insistence the old man turned grudgingly to face her. She saw both resentment and fear in his expression.

"How would I know her? I was a boy o' sixteen."

"But she lived in Amber." Margot raised her voice against a fresh crescendo of music. "You must have met her constantly. What was she like?" So eager was she for an answer that her hand closed fiercely on Rubidge's arm, making him wince.

"Tell me."

"She was wicked." He jerked himself free and lifted his left hand in a curious, defensive gesture. "She was wicked all right, my ma told me. It was common talk she did for poor Mrs Ava Campion, over at Amberside. Time an' again my mother said, bein' drowned was no better than Bess Tuckett deserved. It was the hand of the Lord struck her down, none other than the hand of the Lord. Anyone who denies that will burn in hell for it, an' that's the truth."

X

THEY WERE SINGING in the street like a band of drunks.

Stoned, thought Margot, as she whirled along with them, drunk on music and their own voices and a sense of having outwitted authority.

She heard her own voice taking up a line of song.

"Contralto, yet?" Chilli Gold's grin floated beside her. "We could use you in Amber." The throng suddenly swung across the road and she found herself borne sideways by her companion.

"No," she said, "I'm going home."

"That's it, love, home to The Ram, to pour libations. God, we were good, weren't we?" His feet executed a complicated shuffle of delight.

"They sang well."

"You sang well. I saw you, and heard. You've a nice voice, but never trained, eh?"

"I've no time for singing."

"Ah, that's bloody silly. Music, the arts, are the source of it all, you know. Before man could calculate and weigh, and measure, he had to learn to write. Before he could learn to write, he had to draw. And before he could draw, he had to sing and dance. We are the root of it all. Eliminate us, and you destroy man's root, his sanity."

Panic struck her at that word. She tried to pull free of Gold's grip, but he had fingers of iron. He and the others swept her past the Wool Hall where the clock showed a quarter past ten; on, past the shuttered shops and the little dark gardens to The Ram where the gold sign hung. And in they all went to the public bar.

There they formed exuberant groups, shouting, laughing and shunting back and forth across the room. Chilli edged Margot to the bar counter and bought her a double whisky.

"Zillah says you're a botanist."

"Yes."

"Where d'you work?"

"I've been with a team in the Amazon basin." Although this time she could not bring herself to rebuff him, the jerk of her head warned him. He said quickly. "We won't talk about you if you don't want to. We'll talk about me. Ask me a question, any question."

She looked at him and her mouth curved in a grudging smile. "You, obviously, are a professional musician."

"I am the one and only Chilli Gold. Don't say you never heard of me." His tone was only half bantering.

"I never heard of you."

"No marks for general knowledge."

"I'm sorry. I've been out of circulation for years. Overseas, and when I came home ... three months ago ... I had fever. I've been in hospital."

"Pop."

"What?"

"Popular music. Live shows and television." He pointed skywards. "I've been up there. But I'm abdicating."

"Why?"

"Gonna teach classical guitar."

"Is there enough money in that?"

"Have money, will teach."

"The music tonight . . ." she hesitated, not quite sure of the idea in her mind. "It's a brilliant cycle. I can see that you have to respect Mr Jecks's talent. . . ."

"Even while hating his guts?" Chilli's strange long eyes mocked her. "He's a one-shot artist, Jecks is. Just the Campion Songs to remember him by, when he's gone; that, and the fact that he's a sharp administrator and can get the choir plenty of bookings."

"Does he live here?"

"Yeah. House in Ringan's Close."

"Where's that?"

"Line of Regency pads behind the church."

"How old is Mr Jecks?"

"In his eighties, I s'pose."

"Retired?"

"Oh yeah, has been for years, but still got a pinkie in the musical pies all over Europe. In his prime, he was a sort of dilettante's impresario. Never a pro, but roped in at a stiff price to launch the talented amateurs, to help with the coronations and festivals—not in London, of course, but in the big provincial centres. He's very . . . knowledgeable." Chilli made the adjective sound a little derogatory.

"Why don't you like him?" she said bluntly.

It was his turn to sidestep. "Randall's all right. A good conductor, make no error."

"Was he born in Amber?"

"I think so."

"So he knew Bess Tuckett?"

Chilli looked at her thoughtfully. "Margot, I wouldn't worry too much about Bess, if I were you. People round here don't like to talk about her."

"Why not?"

He shrugged, swinging her empty glass towards him. "Same again? Warm you up for bed."

46

He moved along the bar to fetch the drinks. Margot stayed where she was. If I get drunk, she thought, it's better than those damn pills. Zombie pills. She leaned an elbow on the rail, and watched Zillah Brown thrusting through the crowd. Zillah's cheeks were rosy and her mop of hair more tangled than ever. Like a beautiful witch. Witches were ducked in the old days, if they floated they were guilty, and you stoned them to death. If they sank, they were innocent, but dead anyway. Nowadays, one burned them alive in the yellow press.

Zillah was smiling at her.

"I saw you talking to Ned Rubidge in the church. Did he tell you anything?"

"Yes." Margot gathered her skittering wits. "That Bess did for Mrs Ava Campion."

"What?" Zillah could hardly hear above the noise in the taproom.

"Killed . . ." began Margot, and then found herself displaced at the bar by a large woman whom she recognised as the chief soprano. As the next surge of the human tide carried her back to anchor, Zillah caught her wrist.

"Now. Tell me."

"He said Bess Tuckett deserved to be drowned, because she did for Ava Campion."

"Ned has a wicked tongue when he's drunk. He'll say anything to attract attention."

"I don't think he wanted mine," said Margot, remembering the old man's evasions. "He wasn't really drunk. He was dead scared."

At this point Chilli Gold appeared. It was clear he'd heard at least part of their conversation for he was looking both pensive and wary. Zillah spoke directly to him.

"I warned you, Chilli. You can't use Ned, he's too unstable."

47

"Use for what?" Margot felt their sharpening gaze on her.

They seemed to reach an unspoken decision. Zillah headed for the far side of the room, still towing Margot by the wrist. Chilli followed. They found Ned Rubidge sitting alone at a corner table. His face was shining scarlet and his pale eyes glittered. Whatever his condition had been in the church, he was now pot-valiant.

Chilli slid into the chair opposite him.

"How about a song, Ned?"

"What song d'yer want?"

" 'The Ballad of Ava Campion'."

"Dunno that one."

"It's all right Ned, that's the parson's wife standing there behind you. Bess won't come near while she's around."

The old man laughed raucously. "I don't bother about Bess. Whore, she was, and gone to hell. Seventeen she was, when she took up wi' Jerome Campion, who was old enough to be 'er grandad."

"Hardly. He wasn't fifty when he died. Do you remember what she was like?"

Ned's answer was disconcerting. "A black woman." His strong, wrinkled hands described a series of twists round his shoulders. "Black as coal."

"You mean her hair?"

"An' eyes. Black eyes so fine and big, and a fine big body to go with 'em. Kept a garden, out at the farm. Growed all she needed for 'er physickin'."

"Did she physic Ava Campion?"

" 'Course she did!" Rubidge tilted back his chair and grinned lopsidedly at his audience. "Sixteen when 'er folks died. Seventeen when Jerome started to visit at Tuckett's Farm and no one believed his tale of helpin' with the runnin' of it. An' eighteen when she starts to call at

Amberside, cool as you please, with draughts for poor Mrs. Campion."

"Wait a moment." Zillah had come round to sit at the table. "That must have been in ... what ... 1909? There were doctors in Amber by then."

" 'Course. Dr Wolpert for one, an' others from London too. But there was nothin' they could do for the poor lady. So Bess came with the muck she brewed, and Ava Campion took it. Loved Bess like a daughter and paid dear for it. My mother warned the doctors, but they said let Mrs Campion have what eased her, the stuff was only herb tea, and no harm in it. No harm! My mother goes in one mornin' and there she finds her lady dead on the floor, an' a look on 'er face of such pain you can't imagine. I was at the funeral, so were we all. I saw 'em. Ava's son Dicky Campion on one side o' the grave, with 'is fiancy. Jerome Campion on the other, and be'ind 'im Bess Tuckett, dressed all in black, the lyin' bitch. Got what she wanted, or so she thought. Boasted she'd marry Jerome. Saw the way clear to Amberside, no doubt, but she never lived to travel it. Dead and buried 'erself in six months time, as God willed. May she rot."

"What happened to her and Jerome?"

"River got 'em. We fished 'em out way down beyond Tatley, that's more'n twenty mile. Floods were so bad that year I reckon it was luck they din't go clear out to sea."

Margot, who had remained standing, now set her hands on the table. The second whisky was buzzing in her head, the roar of voices in the taproom was at crescendo, and yet she felt herself to be speaking from a pool of quiet. "Did you see them die?"

Rubidge's head jerked round. "No, I never."

"And your mother? Did she see?"

The question brought a vehement answer. Rubidge threw his weight forward so that the front legs of his chair crashed to the ground. He surged to his feet, roaring incoherently and flailing his arms. His grandson came scurrying from behind the bar, and with Chilli's help got the old man out of the taproom, but they could hear him shouting all the way up the back stairway to his own room.

XI

FOUR WHISKIES DID not equal one sleeping-tablet.

Far from being sleepy, Margot was feverishly awake. She could feel the pounding of her own blood and it was curiously akin to the throb of the river that filled the silent house.

Her head seemed to swell, the sheets burned. She sweated and at once her nightdress wrapped her in ice. She pulled it off and lay shivering.

At half-past two she switched on her light.

In the looking-glass opposite the foot of her bed, she saw her enemy, sitting with raised knees, shoulder and naked breast slick with sweat, hair lank, mouth puckered.

"You're a pretty sight!"

"I'm ill. I should be in hospital."

"Go then, go find one. What sort would you like? A lunatic asylum?"

"I have a fever. The doctors said it might recur. They said I should take care."

"What you have is not fever, it's funk. Want to chicken out, don't you, even if it means being locked up for the rest of your life?"

"That's not fair!"

"Fair? Fair? Who told you life was fair? Move, can't you, slimy creature, slug, get your pills! Move!"

It took her minutes to find the bottle of capsules. She shook one into her hand, went to the bathroom and fetched a glass of water. Drank it down. She ran the basin full of warm water and sponged herself down, dried and powdered and put on a clean nightdress. She was trembling now as if every muscle was at stretch. She found her robe and put it on, pushed her feet into slippers, picked up the quilt from the end of the bed and turned the armchair to face the window. As always, action itself helped to quell her panic. She sat in the chair and leaned back. Cold air flowed about her, touching her forehead and throat. She tucked the quilt about her.

It was a fine night. A spatter of stars showed above Cobbledick Hill. The flooded river raced in a thick coil under the belly of the bridge, to boil white across the ford.

She had always loved to watch water. Streams and torrents, cascades, the sea, had always had power to ease her. Sometimes, on her journeys with Patrick, the craving for a fixed home with stability and children had become unendurable. Then she had gone away by herself and watched water flow, letting it carry grief and frustration away with it.

Jordan. Styx. Death itself was a river, conclusive and all-healing. So why could one not succumb to it? To be dead like Bess Tuckett, rolled down to Tatley or clear out to sea, beyond recall. Dead with her lover. Had she wanted that, had it seemed the best solution?

Suddenly it seemed to Margot that she understood Bess Tuckett; not with any objective understanding, but subjectively, as if her own life and that of the other were superimposed. She knew that Bess had not welcomed death, but had fought against it, in rage and terror. She shared the very sensation of drowning, felt the blows of

52

the floodstream, the battering of rocks and of water that hurled her onward, the taste of mud in her throat.

She flung up her arms in instinctive reaction, and found herself standing upright with the quilt tangled about her feet. Outside, the river Amber kept up its swollen, relentless drumming. On its wooded banks, nothing stirred.

Margot picked up her bedside clock. It was ticking steadily, and its hands showed ten past three, so she could not have slept.

What she had experienced was not a dream, but something from her own mind; or rather, through her own mind. The source lay elsewhere.

She laid fingers on her left wrist. Her pulse was fast, but steady.

She walked over to the mirror. The face there expressed a startled interest. Thin, pale features, and grey-blue eyes, nothing like the "black woman" of Ned Rubidge's description, nobody to see but Margot Wootten.

Yet only a few moments before ... Bess Tuckett ...

It was extraordinary, how little afraid she was. She felt rested, she felt good, better than she had for weeks.

She did not question herself further. She straightened the tumbled bed-clothes, took off her robe and climbed between the sheets. She fell asleep almost at once.

XII

At BREAKFAST THE next morning, Margot was the only guest in the dining-room. She ordered sausage, eggs and fried tomato, but before she had disposed of them, Mrs Rubidge came to stand beside her table.

"Could I speak to you, Mrs Wootten?"

"Of course. Sit down. Have some coffee."

"Nothing, thank you. I just wanted to say I'm sorry about last night."

"Sorry for what?"

"The way Grandfather shouted at you. He wasn't himself."

"He was a little drunk, and so was I. If I'd been sober I wouldn't have asked impertinent questions."

"You meant no harm, did you?"

"So please forget the whole thing."

Still Mrs Rubidge did not move away. Margot regarded her with some interest. Plain she might be, and clumsy, but she was competent. It didn't take long to discover that it was she who ran the inn, not her moon-faced husband. Probably she ran a number of village matters too. There was a shrewd gleam in her eye.

"Do please sit down, Mrs Rubidge, and tell me what's on your mind."

The other complied. "I'm worried about the old man.

If you were thinking of speaking to anyone about him . . ."

"Why ever should I?"

"I just thought . . . you might."

"Look, what happened was a small incident. Unimportant."

"I mean, what happened at the church. Between him and Mr Jecks."

"But that has nothing whatever to do with me."

Mrs Rubidge was silent, tracing patterns on the white tablecloth. Then, "Grandfather says you asked a lot of questions."

"At the church, you mean?"

"Yes. He didn't say what about."

"Nothing important."

"I wondered . . . I thought maybe Mr Campion sent you."

"Who?"

"Mr Niall Campion. To find things out."

"Never heard of him. I spoke to Mr Rubidge about Bess Tuckett."

"Bess . . . ?" Mrs Rubidge looked first startled, then comprehending. "Well, that explains why he got so excited. I mean it's red rag to a bull."

"Do you know why?"

"No. Just is."

Margot poured herself more coffee. "It's an interesting story. I'd like to know the truth of it."

Something like anger touched the long leporine face opposite her. "I don't think you'll get that, Mrs Wootten."

"Why not?"

"They won't like you meddling."

"Who won't?"

"The Campions, for one."

"And your grandfather, for another?"

"My grandfather has good reasons."

"I'm sure. But I'd have to know them, before I decided to keep my counsel, which is what you're asking me to do, isn't it?"

Mrs Rubidge began an angry retort, then seemed to think better of it. "He hates Bess Tuckett. It's no wonder, when you think of the harm she brought his own mother."

"You're not suggesting Bess poisoned her, too?"

"No, no, how could that be? Bess died long before. But I'll have to tell you the whole of it, or as much as I know. It's only hearsay, and what I've picked up over the years, for old Ned will never talk of it.

"His mother, Edith, was widowed young. She had only the one son, and nothing saved when her husband died. She was desperate for a place where she could work and make a home for the boy. Ava Campion gave her a post at Amberside.

"Edith was housemaid, then parlourmaid, then she became Mrs Campion's own dresser, which was a well-paid position, and she had nice rooms in the house for herself and Ned. You can imagine the difference that made to them, being able to stay together, and want for nothing. The Campions were good church people, like Edith. There were prayers every morning for the whole household, and church twice on Sunday if they could manage it. Edith had always been very religious, but when she went to Amberside she kind of threw herself into praying and the Bible and talk of salvation. I've often thought that must have been the first sign of her trouble, though no doubt she was only looking for comfort in her need.

"There's some people that can carry religion, and some that can't. Mrs Campion, now, was three-quarters of the way to being a saint. You look round Amber and you'll see what she gave. The chapel, the school buildings, the new wing for the Wool Hall. And she was loved, which is

56

more'n you can say for most Holy Hannahs. Edith loved her, that's certain.

"It happened there was a good way for her to prove how she felt, because Mrs Campion was delicate. She had a bad heart, and needed a lot of care. Edith never spared herself to give it, and you'll agree, when you put your heart and soul into looking after someone, you can come very close to them.

"I suppose Edith must have felt jealous when Bess Tuckett came along, and took over a lot of the little tasks that Edith had done. Mrs Campion just seemed to be under a spell, the way she allowed Bess the freedom of the house, and swallowed whatever medicine was handed to her, although it was common gossip that Bess was setting her sights on Jerome Campion.

"Edith tried to warn Mrs Campion, I've no doubt, but there's not much a servant can say against a favoured guest, specially when their job's everything they own in the world. Edith had to stand back and watch what went on without being able to prevent it. My grandfather told me once that around that time he often saw his mother praying, as if it was all she knew to do.

"Still nobody thought Bess would harm Mrs Campion. It came as a terrible shock when Edith went in one morning and found the poor thing dead. There were doctors to hand, who said it was her heart. Everyone took it as that. It was only Edith who thought otherwise, at first, but she didn't dare speak out.

"Months later, though, the true story began to be told. People began to recall there were odd things happened the night Mrs Campion died. Everyone could see how, now she was out of the way, Bess and Jerome were in each other's pockets. The talk grew. It must have been terrible talk. Murder, that's a terrible thing. It played on Edith's mind. Well, you can understand how it would. Feeling as

57

she did about Mrs Campion, and not being able to save her, being religious and bound to speak evil of no one ... it must all have been a dreadful strain on her mind.

"Then Bess was drowned, and Jerome with her. There were plenty who saw it as a judgement."

"And Edith Rubidge? What became of her?"

"She went out of her head. It wasn't a sudden thing. Religious mania, and the doctors had a long name for it, she was near fifty when they had to have her locked up, and she died in the home not long after. You can say it would have happened anyway. Or you can blame Bess Tuckett, as we do, for being the cause of so much misery."

"So Bess is dead, but not forgotten?"

A look both stubborn and evasive closed upon Mrs Rubidge's face. "We don't dwell on it. It's not healthy to dwell on things like that. Best to forget them, as you should do, Mrs Wootten."

XIII

It NOW BEING well after nine, Margot walked across the road to Asher's Garage. In the roadway outside it, a lad in overalls was polishing a brand-new Lamborghini. The space round the petrol pumps was empty and Margot, seeing no sign of Will Asher in the glass-fronted office, wandered into the workshop beyond.

The shed was L-shaped, quite large, with three inspection pits. Her own Fiat was in the short arm at the back, tucked behind an enormous tractor. She examined it briefly, noticing that it had been cleaned and polished as well as serviced; and then, wanting to take her book of maps from the cubby-hole, she climbed into the passenger seat.

She found the book and opened it to the page showing East Amber. While she was studying this, she heard Will Asher's voice, raised in obvious anger, coming from the far side of the tractor.

"What I sing and how I sing it is my affair, Mr Campion, and that's a fact."

"You don't heed your own choirmaster, evidently!" The second voice was calm and fluting, tinged with amusement.

"We give respect where it's due—to talent, not blather ... but there's right and wrong in music, same as elsewhere. Which you'd likely not understand."

"Oh, I make no claim to musicianship. What concerns me is hard cash. Like a number of other people, I have put a great deal of money into promoting the Amber Festival, and I don't care to see it put in jeopardy by an *agent provocateur* like Chilli Gold."

"Chilli is a musician. You listen to him, and you won't lose by it."

"My dear Asher, my listening to the views of a pop singer won't alter the central fact, that Randall Jecks is essential to the smooth running of the Festival. He has a contract with the Festival Board, and that contract gives him the right to train the Amber choir and direct it as he sees fit. I don't need to tell you that if the terms of the contract are broken by the indiscipline of you chaps, old Randall could pull out, and not only cost us a deal of money, but quite wreck this year's arrangements with any number of visiting artists, orchestras, and patrons. You must remember that."

"We did remember it, Mr Campion. We read the contract, and we asked advice on it, too. . . ."

"Indeed? From whom?"

"No need for you to worry about that. A good lawyer, that's who, and his advice was there was nothing to make us sing a bloody note for Jecks if we didn't want to. That's a bum contract you've got yourselves. 'Course, you can fire the lot of us, if you like, and get a new choir. No skin off our nose."

"You know perfectly well that's impossible, at this stage. I must say, I find it incredible that you can put so much at risk, simply because you want to perform some silly song in a new way. Why not accept Randall's ruling for the moment? Once the Festival is over, you can sing it backwards for all I care. Isn't that the sensible way to look at it?"

"It is—if all you care for is the money."

"I don't like your attitude, Asher."

"Then y'can stuff it, Campion."

There was a moment's total silence broken by the second voice, now shrill with rage.

"I must remind you that I can make things very difficult for you. Don't imagine you'll get any of the repairs from my factory, in future."

"Suits me. I'm tired of carrying your bad debts, anyways. Now, if you don't mind, I've work to do."

There was the sound of footsteps receding towards the door. Margot hesitated, and then climbed out of the Fiat and walked round the tractor.

"Mr Asher?"

Will swung round to face her. His long face was flushed. "Did you hear that little twister?"

"Yes, I'm sorry, I couldn't help it."

"Bloody threatenin' me." Asher seemed to care little for the ethics of eavesdropping. "Jecks 'as been after 'im, take my word."

"Because of the Campion Cycle?"

"Not as simple as that. Never is, is it? Look, the Campions own half the land that side of the river, and Jecks owns a fair slice this side. Gives 'em ideas above their station, see? This isn't the bloody feudal age. But a property owner can still push people about. Campion wants to turn the old Amberside estate into a factory site, but that's arable land, and we stepped in and got the County to say 'no'. Now he's sniffin' round, right here in Amber. Like us all out, no doubt. Well, he won't get that, either, because the Historic Monuments says not."

Margot, not very interested in this rural land-grabbing, tried to turn the stream. "What's Mr Campion's first name?"

"Niall."

"What relation to Jerome Campion?"

"Grandson. Jerome's boy Dicky was killed in the First World War. This is the son."

"Does he live here?"

"No, London. Down for the weekend, most likely, staying with 'is mum. Mrs Ianthe Campion."

"She must be very old."

"Over eighty."

"Does she live at Amberside?"

"No, no 'At's closed up. Lives in the Dower House an' lucky if she doesn't have to pay rent for it. Niall even tried to make us rent the barn, last Festival. After Jerome left it to Amber in perpetuity. Don't need to tell us to read the small print when Niall's around."

Will's fury had ebbed as he spoke, and he wore his former taciturn look. Directing a nod at the Fiat, he said, "Well, Mrs Wootten, there she is, ready whenever you need her."

"I thought I might stay over till Monday."

"Well, roads'll be clearer then. I'll have her taken over to The Ram for you, you're entitled to free garagin' there and there's less chance of some fool bashin' into her if she's under lock an' key. She's a nice little car."

Margot paid for the work done, by cheque. When she left the garage, she did not return to the inn, but walked on towards the centre of the village.

She had intended to call at the vicarage, but as she passed the supermarket, Zillah Brown emerged with her arms full of groceries, and her two sons in tow.

XIV

MARGOT MOVED TOWARDS them.

"I was going to call on you. . . ."

"Were you? Good!" Zillah peered at her closely. "Are you feeling all right, Margot? You look a bit feverish."

"It's nothing. I had typhus a while ago and it takes time to get over it."

The younger boy fixed her with a clinical stare. "Is typhus the same as typhoid?"

"No. You get typhus from being bitten by a louse."

"Where did you get it?"

"South America. At the mouth of the Amazon."

"I saw that, once, on telly. It was yech."

"So is typhus."

"Do you have convulsions?"

"Ben," interjected his mother, "don't pester Dr Wootten."

"I was only showing an appropriate concern."

"You are a nosey parker, that's what. Now you and Roley can take these things home. Leave them on the kitchen table and I'll sort them later. Okay?"

"Can we have 50p for torch batteries, please?"

Zillah gave them the money, handed over her packages, and watched them disappear into the alley alongside the supermarket. Then she smiled at Margot.

"Was it me you wanted to see, or Coker?"

"You."

"We can't talk on the pavement. Let's go over to the Wool Hall."

They crossed the main street and Woolmarket square, a fine cobbled space with a pilgrim's cross at the centre. On the north side lay the guild-hall that Margot had noticed on her first day in Amber. A handsome facade carried the date 1652. The matching wings on the left and right had been built, Zillah said, by Jerome Campion.

"He meant it to house the Festival offices, and a small auditorium. He had dreams of building something really big, later on, for opera. Seems crazy now, but it wasn't, then. I suppose there was more money, and more leisure for music. Amber had a good name among musicians. Randall Jecks could tell you about all that. Then Jerome died, and his son Richard was killed in the war. That left only Ianthe. She couldn't give a darn for music."

"She still lives here, I'm told."

"Yes, over the river."

"Do you know her?"

They had reached the main entrance, and passed through it into a wide foyer, Caroline in style, with a flagged floor. At the back was a bay with benches for patrons. Zillah led the way across to the nearest.

"Ianthe?" she said as she settled herself. "Nobody really knows Ianthe Campion. Coker and I are asked to dinner at the Dower House once a year. She comes regularly to church. She's a good subscriber to charity. But we're on different planes."

"You mean she's a snob?"

"No. She doesn't care what people think of her. It's not that she thinks herself above us. More as if she's not focused on us at all. She's like a camera that's jammed so

64

that all it can register is something far away. Of course, she's old. . . ."

"What does the lens register?"

"A dead sort of world. She was a famous hostess—not in the way the Campions had been. She held parties here, and in France. A couple of years ago, she sold a stack of jewels, and there were stories in the papers, how she'd worn a sapphire parure when Edward VII visited Amberside, stuff like that. And fashion, clothes, the right places at the right time. It's all rather boring." Zillah shook her yellow curls. "Perhaps her trouble is that she's bored with everything."

"Is she short of money?"

"Not by my standards, but it's relative, isn't it?"

"Does she share her son's business interests?"

"I'd say, not at all. She's rather stupid, you know."

"And Niall?"

"Not stupid at all. A smart alec. His idea is to demolish all the old buildings in Amber and develop the area for industry. As if there isn't plenty of land to the south, for that! He's got half the council in his pocket, too, and he pulls strings all round the county. . . ."

"You're trying to stop him?"

For the first time, Zillah looked evasive.

Margot said, "I was in Asher's Garage half an hour ago. I overheard Niall Campion trying to pressurise Mr Asher into doing what Randall Jecks wants."

"He won't get far with Will."

"And there's a Festival Board, I gather."

"Yes, Niall is chairman of that. Jerome left a request that a member of his family be invited to sit on the Board, and it's always been honoured. The way the Board's constituted, we . . . the parish of Amber . . . elect half the members. That's ten. Another five are co-opted for their special knowledge of music. Randall Jecks is one of those.

65

And five are nominated by the Campion family, that means Ianthe and Niall. The Board was supposed to provide the financial and cultural backing for the Festival. Since Niall came on the scene six years ago, he's slowly got rid of the people who want to promote music, and got in people who want to promote themselves. They see the Amber Festival as a way to attract trippers. And that's disgusting. Amber's always been a place for musicians. We've been making musical instruments for centuries. Most of the people you heard singing last night are descended from skilled craftsmen.... Come into the hall, I'll show you."

They went through folding doors to a long and lofty chamber panelled in linen-fold oak. Along the rear wall of this was fastened a mighty board, emblazoned with gilt, and carved with many names.

"There!" Zillah pointed. "This was the headquarters of a guild, remember. Wool was their trade, but music was their craft and that list honours the members of the guild who made a special contribution to music. Joseph Hogg, skin-merchant. His firm still finds the best skins for drumheads in this part of the country. Roger Qwilt—he sang before George III, who probably didn't enjoy it much. Ebrim Goodstone, choirmaster, Matthew Tuckett, lute-maker, Samuel Hogg, 'who paid such sums as would hire for ten years a boy to pump the organ'...that's in the parish history. Music mattered to all these men, and it matters now. If we can build up the Festival into something good, then we'll be doing a favour to ourselves and a whole lot of other people. It would keep Amber alive...."

"Is it dying?"

Zillah frowned. "Coker says that a place survives only as long as it fulfils a human need. When the wool trade declined, so did Amber. We can't bring that back, but we can revive music."

Margot, thinking of her visit to Tuckett's Farm, said, "Was it only a matter of wool? I mean, those people who repaired musical instruments, why did they leave? They can't all have been wool-merchants."

"I don't know. There was an exodus. Perhaps it was the Great War. Anyway," she repeated vehemently, "we can bring the skills back, we can do useful, creative work ... if we can get rid of that damned ring of fat-cats round Niall."

"Where does Randall Jecks stand on revivals?"

"He's another sharpie." Zillah seemed suddenly to recollect her rôle as minister's wife. "I shouldn't talk like this, but he makes me mad. He's clever, and knows how to train a choir. But he's eighty-two years old and a mass of vanity. He plays along with Niall, and runs to him for support if he's crossed. I don't know why I'm telling you all this. It's none of your worry."

"Perhaps it should be," said Margot. She glanced up and encountered her companion's puzzled gaze. She answered it obliquely.

"I arrived here by chance. I didn't have any planned destination. Just drove. I ran out of petrol on Cobbledick Hill. When the tank's empty, the place where you stop is the place of at least one decision ... how to get it filled."

"Are you ... ?" began Zillah, then changed her mind. "I have the feeling I know your face. Are you someone famous?"

"No." Margot turned away abruptly.

"Sorry!"

"No, don't you apologise. I should. I'm simply ... not myself." At the words, she found herself listening for that other voice that was always so ready to seize upon the smallest weakness ... plead and wheedle for surrender ...

67

but for once it was silent. There was only Zillah, bending towards her.

"Are you sure you're all right?"

"Perfectly. There's something else I want to tell you. Nancy Rubidge spoke to me this morning. She talked about the death of Ava Campion."

She told Zillah the story as it had been told to her.

XV

THE WEATHER HAD cleared during the morning, and in the afternoon a mild sunlight flooded the head of Cobbledick Hill. Margot approached the girl at the reception desk.

"Is it possible to visit Amberside?"

"You could drive into the grounds and walk round it, like, but it's all locked up."

"Does no one live there?"

"Not now, no. There's Jarrett to keep an eye on things, but even so the windows get broken."

"Do I need permission?"

"No. There's plenty of people go up the woods for picnics. There's nice walks, too. But wear old shoes, it'll be mud to your ankles."

Margot sought directions and was given them, and by two thirty was edging the Fiat along a much-neglected lane through the woodland. This must have been fine once, but now the thickets had encroached among the boles of elm and beech, and saplings sprang in the park. There was a dried-up lake, a folly on a hillock, and finally, at a sudden turn, Amberside itself. Margot stopped the car to look her fill.

The house, though not of Palladian magnificence, was very large indeed. Three-storeyed, built of red brick with a white stone centrepiece, it was somehow Italianate in style. The roof was flat, with a stone balustrade running right round it, and this was matched by a wide terrace stretching the whole length of the ground level.

An effect of solidity, power and determination which Margot found a little daunting.

She drove on, circling the building, until she came to a wide open space at its rear. Overgrown paths and a sundial indicated this must have been a small garden. Margot left the car and wandered towards a bank of lavender bushes, of the French and English varieties. She found fennel growing, and mint, rosemary and marjoram. A herb garden, which had been well tended until quite recently.

Bess Tuckett might have gathered some of her simples here, but not yew or saffron, oleander or nicotina. No poison.

These thoughts were interrupted by the sound of a voice, singing lustily.

Over to the left was a thicket of rhododendrons and beyond that the roof of a stable, complete with clock tower. The singing came from that direction. Margot headed towards it.

The stables must have been built at the same time as the house. The bricks were of the same colour, and had been put together with the same air of determination; but because this structure was small and functional, the onlooker was not cowed, but reassured.

There were a dozen closed doors, presumably loose boxes, with lofts over them; two sets of carriage-doors, and above those, a balcony from which one might reach the coachman's quarters. The singer was on the balcony.

Margot started up the stairway, but stopped halfway.

At the top of the steps, in a patch of sunlight, stood a copper bath-tub, marvellously embossed with nymphs and tritons. Sitting in the tub was Chilli Gold.

He stopped singing at sight of Margot, tilted his head, grinned, and lifted a hand in greeting.

"Forgive my not getting up."

"What are you doing here?"

"I live here. Bed, sit but no bath."

"H and C laid on?"

"Only at horse level." Chilli reached up to the wooden handrail, hooked a towel towards him, and draped it round himself as he rose from the foam. "Wait while I dress. Won't be a moment."

He emerged minutes later in jeans and jersey, ran down the stairs, and put an arm round Margot's shoulders. She stepped away from him.

"How do you empty the bath water?"

"Drink it."

"Where is Mr Jarrett?"

"In the hayloft. Come up and I'll introduce you."

"I don't believe he's here at all."

"Quite right. It's his afternoon off. Can't I help you?"

Margot considered him. There was a glint in his eye that was watchful as well as amused. He had the smile, she thought, of the Etruscan statues; three-cornered, ribald, a little cruel. She said uncertainly:

"They told me Jarrett was caretaker here."

"So he is. Did you want to see Amberside?"

"Yes."

Chilli shrugged. "If that's all. . . ." He turned away and vanished round the corner of the stables. When he returned, he was carrying a large bunch of keys.

"Come along, love."

"Is it all right to use those?"

"Sure. I spent the whole of last summer escorting visitors round. Better than the guide-books, honest."

"So the place hasn't been closed long?"

"About eight months."

"But I thought. . . ."

"The position is this. In 1946, when Niall came back from the army, his mother was in the Dower House, and there was a school here at Amberside. It took several years to get the school shifted, and by the fifties everyone knew the Toad Halls of the world were a dead loss . . . from the private occupier's angle. Niall kept a few rooms open, but never lived here. He had caretakers. In summer, he allowed groups to tour, and turned the park into a caravan site. He decided this year to shut it up altogether, and try and get permission to demolish, so that he could build a factory. It was thrown out, but he's still battling."

They had reached a door in the east wall. The mass of the building towered over them, oppressive even in sunlight. The door unlocked, they passed into the dark and musty atmosphere of a house long closed. Chilli led the way through corridors and intervening rooms, to an enormous hallway, two storeys high, and composed, it seemed, entirely of marble.

"Deep freeze," he said, and, advancing to the centre of the floor, he stood there in the attitude of the professional guide.

"And now, ladies and gents, we are in the entrance hall to Amberside, the very hall where Rysbrack designed the chimney-piece, as you see a very masterful work, and two statues of note, one thought to be of the school of Bernini. Over the fire-place is the portrait by Sir Joshua Reynolds of Mr Horace Campion who died very sudden of a cerebral apoplexy."

There were of course no statues and no portraits, though the fading of tiles and walls showed where these must have been positioned. Yet Chilli's words created an illusion, if only for a moment, of a place inhabited and alive. He put out a hand to Margot. "Come on, there's more to see."

On they went, through the saloons of the ground floor, and the long, shadowed dining-room. Up a carved staircase to the first floor. Through a ballroom with plastered ceiling, a drawing-room, to a charming oval music-room.

"Pretty," said Margot.

"And effective." Chilli walked to the far end, turned, and spoke in his natural tones. "The acoustics are perfect. Probably the Campion songs were rehearsed for the first time in this room."

He began to hum a snatch of tune. Something prickled Margot's spine and she said sharply, "Don't!"

He made no answer, but stretched out an arm and opened a narrow door set in the white panels. Bowing, he held it for her, and she passed through.

They had reached a second, obviously private stairway, that climbed past a tall window. The surrounding walls were hung with silk brocade, once green, now faded to lime, and disfigured by countless scribbles and chips.

Chilli touched the fabric. "Schoolkids," he said, and started up the stairway. Half way up, he stopped.

"Coming?"

Margot hesitated on the landing. Somehow she did not want to go with him. The light filtering through the window cast a dappled camouflage, so that his face seemed to float and flicker.

"It's nothing," he said softly. "An empty house...."

But was it empty, she thought, as she followed him up? She felt the pressure of so many people in these rooms ... not schoolchildren, that would have been pleasant, but the others ... Jerome and his ailing wife ... Bess Tuckett, and Edith Rubidge, already obsessed....

Library, bedrooms, corridors, endless and cold, ice-cold. They came at last to what must have been the master bedroom, at the front of the house. Margot stood at the main window, from which she had a sweeping view of

Cobbledick Hill, the woods, and the river. She could see the bridge and the surge of floodwater below it. There was the glint of sun on foam, it was daylight, broad daylight, so how was it that she looked at darkness, how was it she heard the clamour of so many voices and above that someone screaming, screaming . . . ?

She threw herself backwards, crashing into Chilli. His hand came up and closed over her mouth, he slammed her towards him.

"Shut up, shut up, Margot, you fool, it's all right!"

She realised it was her own voice screaming, and stopped. Above her head, Chilli muttered, "God almighty. Let's get out of this."

He hustled her down the corridor, down the stairs, away from the dead rooms and out into blessed air. Her knees were buckling and she trembled violently. Chilli pulled her across to a stone bench and they sat down. He took out a handkerchief and wiped her forehead and neck with it.

"So what was all that about?"

"Did I scream first?"

"Well, honey, I certainly didn't."

"But outside . . . at the river, there was someone . . . didn't you hear it?"

"No." He put the hanky away and leaned his palms on his knees, staring at her.

She said, "I'm not crazy. You think I'm crazy, don't you?"

"No. Tell me what happened."

She sat still, picking at a cushion of moss on the stone beside her.

"I was standing there . . . in that room . . . and I felt I knew it. I knew the view from that window. I was looking at the sun on the river, but I saw the river at night. I knew that I was watching the river at night, and waiting for something to happen. I heard people running, and a woman

74

screaming. It wasn't myself, it came from the river. I swear."

"But you did scream, Margot."

"But that was after!" She put out cold hands and grasped Chilli's wrist. "I screamed to . . . wake myself, I had to get away. If I hadn't turned away that moment, I'd have seen Bess Tuckett drowned!"

It seemed to Margot, once she had said these words, that the quality of the silence all about them changed. It was as if the neglected woods, the encroaching shrubs, the high blank façade of the house, turned towards her; and something ominous took a step closer.

She cried out wildly. "I think I'm going out of my mind."

Chilli shook his head. "If you are, then so am I."

"What?"

"I tell you, girl. That room got me, too. Not for the first time." He bent over and pulled a blade of grass and sat twirling it between his fingers. "Last year," he said, "last summer, when I was doing the tours, I was up there along with a whole crowd of people, and they were goofing about, and I went to the window. Stood there, looked out, same as today. And it came to my mind, 'from this window, you could have watched Jerome Campion drowning.' Now why? Association of ideas, maybe. But I've caught fish in that stream, why didn't I think of that?" He looked up at Margot. "Today, I remembered, and I took you up there, wondering whether you'd feel it too. I'm sorry."

"Chilli, you're not just saying that . . . ?"

"No. I promise, it's true. Look, you know what I think? I had an eerie experience, last year, and it scared me. I went up there expecting it to happen again. I was standing right next to you, with these thoughts in my head. You

75

picked them up from me. A case of extra-sensory perception."

Margot faced him. "And if I didn't get it from you?"

"Then we're haunted, love, the pair of us. But not insane." He reached out casually and touched her cheek. "Margot, why don't you tell me about yourself?"

For a moment she was tempted to respond. It would be so pleasant to lean forward into his arms, and talk and talk. But before she could speak, the stutter of a motor engine sounded at the edge of the woods, and she saw an ancient Citroën heading up the drive.

Chilli swore to himself, then stood up. "Jarrett," he said. "I have to talk to him. But this is a postponement, not a cancellation, Margot."

He walked with her to the car, shut her into it, and watched while she drove off. She could see him, in the driving mirror, as he turned to greet someone stepping from the Citroën.

XVI

THE NEXT MORNING was Sunday, and she went to church.

As she approached St Ringan's, this time in fair weather, she could see the noble proportions of the west window, and the great strength of the buttressed walls. She wondered if there was a full peal of bells in the tower, for surely Amber, of all places, must have boasted bell ringers once.

What a waste it all was, this huge church, washed up like a dead whale. Crazy world. No place for the craftsman, no time for the opinions of the individual, no villages, and in the cities a merciless crush of people. No wonder people freaked out, joined the zanies, tried to assert themselves by violent and bizarre behaviour.

The service was a spoken Eucharist, held in the Lady Chapel. Margot sat in the back pew. It was a long time since she had attended Communion, and the first time she had heard the new form. She liked it. She did not believe it, any more than she believed in the form of the fairy story. Once upon a time and happy ever after. But as she grew older, she accepted there was a nub of truth in this faith, just as there was in a myth, if one could only get past the semantics.

Coker Brown wore the serenity of priesthood. As she

watched him move through the acts of celebration, his name, and this occasion, together roused a memory in her. Eliot's words:

We must be still and still moving
Into another intensity
For a further union, a deeper communion
Through the dark cold and the empty desolation,
The wave cry, the wind cry, the vast waters
Of the petrel and the porpoise. In my end is my beginning.

If desolation marked the way, there was hope for her yet.

The old woman sitting at the end of the front pew must be Ianthe Campion. She sat upright, and when her turn came to approach the altar, walked with a leisurely grace. She was tall and a little overweight. She knelt unaided to receive the bread and wine. When she came back towards the congregation, she did not glance at their faces, but waited silently at the end of the row, which was blocked by a woman in prayer. The woman rose. Mrs Campion stepped past without word or smile. After the service ended, she left without speaking to Coker.

Margot stood in the sunlight outside the north door, waiting until he was free to address her.

"Good morning, Margot. You look rested. One thing we can supply, at least."

"Good morning. Thank you, I feel better. Zillah didn't come?"

"No, she's taken the boys over to Colchester today, to my parents. Is there anything I can do?"

How nice he was, asking no questions, beyond the commonplace ones, while his eyes measured her desperate need. He frowned a little, as if she were some very delicate structure that might break if he handled it wrongly. She said gruffly,

"I'm better alone, Coker. I have to make my own way."

"Of course."

"But you can tell me, where will I find Randall Jecks?"

"He lives in Ringan's Close. I'll show you."

He led her across the green turf north of the church, to a wicket gate thickly shaded by trees. Beyond lay a short path and two stone steps giving on to a lane.

"That's Ringan's Close," said Coker. "Randall's house is the third one along."

Margot thanked him and went on alone.

The Close was the work of some Georgian architect. From the curve of the roadway the ground sloped gently down towards the river, and on this slope stood six houses, each in its own carefully ordained grounds, yet none like the next. They expressed to perfection the grace and solidity of the period; and to Margot they seemed also to express the individuality she had lately been thinking about.

These must have been the homes of the one-time merchants of Amber. Men who had put down their roots in the town, building in the shadow of the church which was no doubt a central point in their lives.

Margot crossed the road. The first house had a handsome carriageway. The gate-posts were stone, and bore each a carved medallion, showing a fiddle and bow. The gates themselves were padlocked and the garden beyond, though well kept, had an untrodden look. Probably the owners were absent. Perhaps they belonged to the jet set and only came here in high summer.

She put out a hand and touched a medallion. Music again. She had the feeling that this house and garden had heard much music in the past. It seemed to her that she could hear it now, Mozart, no, Haydn, brisk and vigorous in the distance. . . .

She pulled her hand back, sharply. Hallucinations were a symptom of typhus in its early stages, but they did not persist, and it was time she got her imagination under control. She lifted her head. The music was not spectral, but came from farther up the lane. She turned towards it.

The third house in the Close stood nearer to the road than its fellows, and its garden was smaller, but it had the air of being in full occupation. Smoke curled from the chimneys, the windows were brightly burnished, and a Haydn symphony vibrated within it.

Margot banged the knocker twice. After a while, the door was opened by a middle-aged woman, unsuitably dressed in a denim skirt and a Shetland wool cardigan. She scowled at Margot through very thick spectacles.

"Yes?"

"I wonder whether I may see Mr Jecks?"

"Have you an appointment?"

"No."

"Mr Jecks only sees people by appointment."

"I understand. Unfortunately, I'm just passing through Amber. I'm very anxious to talk to him."

"What about?" The woman sounded both offensive and unsure. Margot, trying to guess her rôle in the household, put it down as cook-disciple. She phrased her next sentence accordingly.

"Could you explain to the maestro that I am greatly interested in the Amber Festival, and particularly in the Campion Cycle?"

"Are you from the press, then?"

"No. My name is Wootten. Dr Margot Wootten." She gave the full title without thinking.

"Doctor of Music?"

"Doctor of Botany, but my father was a Professor of Music, Keith Gering."

The woman's eyelids flickered. It was doubtful if the name of an authority on sixteenth-century church music meant much to her, but she was evidently not anxious to put her ignorance to the test. She said grudgingly, "I'll ask him", and moved off down the hall towards the rear of the house. Margot stood waiting.

The symphony had stopped, leaving a silence so complete that she could hear the wind stirring in the woods behind her. The hall she faced was spacious, with elegant double doors to left and right—reception rooms no doubt —and a white-painted staircase. She was reminded of the houses of Vermont, standing amidst fiery maples. The furnishing was of a later period than the building. There was a big bowl of late roses on a table. No pictures, but a number of framed autographs and opera programmes.

The disciple returned looking piqued.

"He'll see you."

Margot followed her through an archway and then right, along a corridor that backed the entire length of the ground floor. Through a succession of tall windows she glimpsed a lawn, and willows, their long fronds awash in the swollen river. She could hear the roar of the water.

The guide tapped at a door. A voice called, "Enter." They went into a room that had clearly been designed as an auditorium.

At the near end were several rows of gilt and velvet chairs. Others were stacked against walls hung with crimson brocade. In the far left-hand corner was a grand piano, flanked by music stands. In the right-hand corner, arranged in a sort of bay, was a room within a room; a brocaded sofa, two or three little tables, a box ottoman and two large cabinets. Rugs covered the floor and damask curtains were looped back from the window on heavily-tasselled cords. The temperature was oppressively warm.

A splendid enough setting, and in the middle of it, leaning back in a wing chair in a somewhat studied pose, was Randall Jecks.

He rose as the two women entered, and held out a hand to Margot. Was she expected to rush forward and fall on her knees? Instead, she took the hand and found it small, cold, and fragile. Indeed, that rather described the whole man, now that she saw him close to. The long nose and tiny chin, the prominent eyes and shock of white hair, reminded her of the delicate and exotic little fish she had seen in tropical pools. Indeed, an indoor tank stood on a window ledge, flanked by a stand of ferns and a cage of blue parakeets.

"Dr Wootten," announced the disciple.

"Indeed, yes," said Jecks, flashing exceptionally white dentures. "I knew your dear father, not well of course, but by acquaintance, and by his writings. An erudite and musicianly man. Cambridge was the place we first met, and the year ... let me see ... 1935. Before you were thought of. Do please sit down. May I offer you tea?"

"I'd love some."

"Rhoda, my dear? Can you fix?"

When Rhoda had left them, Jecks returned to his place, and sat with his hands on his knees, studying her.

"You were at the rehearsal on Friday evening, were you not?"

"Yes. May I say I enjoyed it very much? You have a really terrific choir."

"They're not bad, not bad. I'm sorry you witnessed that unpleasant little scene. One is rather exasperated by old Ned Rubidge. When he has drink taken, he becomes quite irresponsible."

"Nothing could spoil the impact of your cycle of songs.

I have heard them sung before, of course, but never like they were sung here; with passion and accuracy. It's an unusual combination."

"Ah well, you were getting the thing at source, so to speak." The little man was intelligent enough to know he was being buttered up, but he couldn't resist the flattery. His vanity showed, in the way he bridled. She planted her first dart. "I had never heard it with lute accompaniment."

"As I explained, I did not write it for lute, but for pianoforte."

"The lute had a rightness ... perhaps I'm biased. I love lute music. I'm told many of the finest instruments of the past came from hereabouts."

"Amber had some excellent workmen. I'm afraid the skill is lost."

"With the Tucketts?"

"What?"

"The Tucketts," she repeated. "Wasn't that the family?"

"Yes, that's correct. You have been reading the old histories?"

"No. I was in the Wool Hall yesterday."

"Of course." He had recovered his urbanity. At that moment Rhoda came back with a tray of tea; elaborate silver and Worcester china, thin brown bread and butter, walnut cake, sliced lemon, milk and cream. Another world, pre-war.

Randall Jecks fussed over the teacups, talking as he poured. "Don't misunderstand me, please, when I criticise the actions of certain people at the rehearsal. Young Gold, for instance, is a splendid performer. And I say that despite the pop image. He is also, I'm sorry to say, an *agent provocateur*, like so many of his generation. Born to trouble as the sparks fly upward. It is all because of the Festival, you know. Cream or lemon? There. And a little plate? Now! The idea is to discredit me. I am, after all,

83

old, and age as you realise is a crime these days. Therefore Gold and his cronies lose no opportunity to make me appear reactionary and bad at my job."

"I don't see how they can do that. The choir is obviously extremely well trained."

"Thank you. B and b or cake? Good, good. Yes, I feel I can honestly say I've helped to build the Amber choir, and the Amber Festival, into something rather fine. Now I admit at once that to do that, I have had to pay attention to the purely financial aspects. You know yourself that the music that draws the musician, and the music that draws the popular vote, is not one and the same thing. So I've always tried to salt in what one might call experimental stuff with the tried and true box-office appeal. The same applies to performers. Bring the new names, by all means, but remember that people look for proven worth when they are putting down their money.

"This is what I have tried, time and again, to explain to Chilli Gold, but he doesn't listen. He doesn't want to. He wants to get rid of me, take my place, and turn the Amber Festival into his own sort of circus, no doubt a sort of Woodstock frequented by hippies, guitarists and jazz aficionados."

There was genuine affront in the old man's voice; and really, thought Margot, in an access of contrition, who the hell am I to criticise him? What do I know of the squabbles of this god-forsaken place, what right have I to leech on to them . . . I've got to get out of here. . . .

Randall Jecks was speaking again. "But I bore you with my little problems, I am a poor host. You came with a purpose. So pray, Dr Wootten, what may I do to help you?"

Caught off balance, Margot hesitated. She felt the brief silence become a physical weight; as if, beyond the window, the vista of river and hill listened for a voice not hers, as if here in this room, there was an alien presence.

She spoke without conscious plan.

"Was it really a case of murder, do you think?"

XVII

Randall Jecks stared at her in total lack of comprehension.

"Murder? What murder?"

"I'm sorry. I don't know what made me say that. Ned Rubidge told me on Friday...something about Bess Tuckett...that there was a story she murdered Mrs Campion." Margot pressed her hands to her cheeks. "I've been having nightmares...."

"And no wonder!" Jecks set down his teacup so hard that it tipped over in the saucer. "I told you old Rubidge is quite irresponsible. I suppose he was drunk?"

"Partly."

"There! He likes attention and doesn't mind how much distress his wild stories may cause. Unbalanced, I fear. His mother ended her days in an asylum. You poor child!"

"But it can't just be rumour," said Margot. "There's the tombstone, remember?" As Jecks watched her uneasily, she hurried on. "I happen to be a Doctor of Botany. The day after I arrived, I was wandering round the churchyard and I saw the stone on Bess Tuckett's grave. It shows a carving of plants, all poisonous. And Ned said she killed Ava Campion."

"He certainly wouldn't dare say anything of the kind to me," snorted her host. "What a forked tongue that old

86

devil has!" He straightened his cup. "What you say of the tombstone . . . it's news to me. One doesn't look at these things by choice, and of course poor Bess has been dead over fifty years."

"You don't believe she was guilty?"

"Of murder? Of course not. Of adultery, perhaps. In my young day, you know, adultery was considered almost as serious a crime as murder. But there is no proof that Bess broke any of the commandments."

"Proof aside, do you think she did?"

She was rewarded by a singularly astute glance from the protuberant eyes.

"Why do you ask? The woman is dead. What profit is there in raising her ghost?"

"Has it been laid?"

Jecks said nothing for some time. He refilled Margot's cup, offered her sugar, with the abstracted expression of someone trying to reach a decision. At length he said:

"What you have heard is mere regurgitation of old scandals. I would rather ignore it, but I see that that won't do. I shall tell you the facts, and I hope that as a woman of sense you will draw the right conclusions." He leaned back in the attitude of the raconteur, and ran a hand over his thatch of white hair.

"It was . . . let me see . . . 1910 or so when it began. The Tucketts farmed the land south of the river, farmed it well; it had been in their family for a great many years. Joel and Ellen Tuckett were the owners at that time, and Bess was their only child. She did not favour her parents, but took after her maternal grandmother, an Italian singer who came to Amber with a troupe, married a local man, and stayed. Bess was like her, dark and voluptuous. Also talented. She had a fine contralto voice and a sharp intelligence.

"In 1910 there was an outbreak of fever in this part of

Suffolk, and the Tuckett parents caught it and died, leaving Bess, sixteen years old and with no relatives in England.

"Jerome Campion was the owner of Amberside, across the river from the Tuckett farm. The big house, you may have seen it as you drove into Amber? Yes. Campion was the largest landowner, the local squire at a time when such people had duties to perform. He made it his business to see that the Tuckett girl was not left to fend for herself. Jerome put in some of his own workpeople to set the farm going and tried to arrange for Bess to go to a boarding-school. But she flatly refused to leave home. She was head-strong in the extreme, and peculiarly devoted to her sur-roundings. She loved Amber and its fields and woods, and she had an astonishing knowledge of the indigenous plants. You might say she was a botanist like you, although without your academic training. And there was her voice . . . quite exceptional. . . .

"You knew her?"

"Oh yes. We were born here, grew up in the same village. I was twenty before I left, which makes me roughly the same age as she was. In the year of the epidemic, I had just started at the London School of Music. In the holi-days, I earned what I could, teaching and as an accom-panist. I worked with Bess for a few weeks in the summer of 1911. Her voice was contralto, but with an amazing range, and its timbre was exciting. My main concern was to persuade her not to ruin her chances by overstraining her voice . . . so many do . . . and I encouraged her to take things easily, stick to simple Lieder.

"She was not without backing, Jerome Campion was aware of her musical gifts. I certainly didn't worry unduly about her, having my own career to make. After that summer, I returned to my studies. When I was home again for Christmas, I found that Jerome had become so convinced of the excellence of Bess Tuckett's talent, that he was planning to make a concert singer of her.

"He'd engaged a singing-master ... ostensibly to train the Amber choir, but in fact for Bess. This man was to give her lessons in singing, the pianoforte, history of music, harmony. It is hardly to be wondered at that the village found this concern excessive. Here was Jerome, a man then in his middle forties, with an invalid wife, a man who moved in the best society that London, Paris ... and Amber ... could provide, who was patron of one of Europe's most prestigious music associations, who had great wealth and a beautiful home; and he was devoting all this money, attention and thought to a seventeen-year-old farmer's daughter. It was bound to cause talk. I heard it, that Christmas. I observed Jerome and the girl. I felt he was certainly in love with her, but that there was nothing unsavoury in their relationship.

"I was, as I said, often away from Amber over the next two years. On the rare occasions I was home, with my parents in this house, I met both Jerome and Bess in highly formal circumstances. One was aware of warmth of feeling between them, but it seemed an innocent relationship. They shared a passion for music, and Bess felt for Jerome all the devotion and admiration which a young girl, deprived of parental love and care, must feel for her benefactor and guardian.

"All might have been well, had it not been for the fact that Ava Campion, Jerome's wife, was a desperately ill woman. She was one of those people who seem to suffer from so many physical ailments that the entire system is always on the verge of collapse. In 1909 she suffered a severe illness, pneumonia I think it was, and from then on she was virtually confined to her own home. She endured dreadful attacks of cardiac asthma. It was understood she might go at any time.

"Yet despite her frail constitution, Ava Campion was a most remarkable woman. She had a truly lovable disposition, gentle and considerate for others, far-seeing and humorous. She was always very kind to me, and gave me help and introduced me to people who could serve my career. My father was a wealthy man, but a Philistine. He wished me to become a lawyer, and would not stake a penny for my musical education, but Ava, who was my godmother, paid for all I needed. I felt so beholden that I earned what I could, as I have explained, but of course it was not enough.

"Well, Ava used to lie on her couch in her little sitting-room at Amberside, and somehow manage to keep in touch with the world. She was a great letter-writer. Artists all over the world were her friends and confidants, and the people of this village held her in something very like reverence.

"I think she knew Jerome had fallen in love with Bess, and I think she suffered for him as much as for herself. In those days, people had to put up with such a situation. Jerome would not have dreamed of asking for a divorce, even if there had been grounds for it. He was devoted to Ava and well aware of her qualities.

"You must remember, too, that Amberside was still the centre of a glittering social life. In the time of Edward VII, families like the Campions still had enormous fortunes, and entertained on a princely scale. A glimpse of the visitors' books at the Campion Museum will show you that Amberside was host not only to musical celebrities, but to a cross-section of poets, artists, and statesmen, as well as to all manner of other folk, like me. If it seems strange that a woman as delicate as Ava should act hostess, I can only tell you that she was an important part of the Amberside scene, not only to Jerome but to scores of others. There was no legitimate place there for Bess Tuckett.

"Bess must have lived a lonely life. She had no kin of her own, and her friendship with Jerome had its own built-in loneliness. She was fiercely independent, and did not take kindly to advice, let alone criticism. When she heard it whispered she was trying to break Jerome's marriage, she turned on her denigrators, and attacked them openly. She made enemies. Even moderate opinion was offended by her outspokenness.

"Ava Campion intervened. She took what I still think was a very strange course. She welcomed Bess into her own close family circle, welcomed her at Amberside and made it plain she would hear no word against her.

"Bess began to visit the Campions almost every day. She would walk or ride across the bridge and take the path up through the wood . . . and spend the morning at Amberside, reading to Ava, singing to her, merely chatting.

"Ava had several medical men attending her. There was Dr Wolpert from Kersey, a thoroughly sound man with a large practice; and specialists from London. None of them seemed to do her a ha'porth of good. Medical science was not what it is now, you know.

"I can't tell you at what point Ava decided to try Bess Tuckett's skill as a herbalist. Bess had quite a reputation roundabout for her simples, and you will understand better than I how plants with medicinal properties can be turned to man's aid. . . ."

". . . or to his destruction . . ."

". . . as you say. At any rate, Bess used to prepare tisanes for Ava, things that helped her to sleep, and something for her asthma attacks. Also an infusion that acted as a diuretic, I think. And whether by chance, or by imagination, or by accurate treatment, Ava improved. She was not healed, but she was far more active and com-

91

fortable than she had been for years. She became very attached to Bess, and dependent upon her.

"This rather strange state of affairs was accepted, and for a little while the gossip died down. Things went happily until Ava and Jerome's son, Richard—Dicky as he was known—came down from Cambridge and brought with him his fiancée, Ianthe Fullerton. You may know the family?"

"Not at all."

"Oh, cream of the cream." There was a certain glint of malice in Randall's eye. "Very distinguished, very correct, and quite impossibly dull. Ianthe was a beauty much fêted in London, but somehow she had not married. She was twenty-three, and her two younger sisters were safely wed. Ianthe was shy, perhaps. Rather a prude. She was very much shocked by Bess Tuckett, and as she spent a great deal of time staying with her in-laws-to-be, you can imagine it was not long before she and Bess fell out. I have often wondered if Ava encouraged them to quarrel. She didn't think Ianthe was right for her boy, and perhaps hoped to edge her off, or make Dicky change his mind.

"Bess, being Bess, was insufferable towards Ianthe. She used to make fun of her. Poor Ianthe had no ear for music and not much sense of humour. She once mistook Baa Baa Black Sheep for the slow movement of Schubert's Unfinished, so that gives you an idea. . . .

"By the summer of 1912, life at Amberside was very difficult. Ianthe was refusing to speak to Bess. Ava was making it clear she would not take sides. And when I came home for the vacation, I realised that Bess, whatever had been her earlier feelings, was now in love with Jerome, head over heels in love and typically quite reckless. It was torturing her, and at the same time she was happy. Perhaps she was his mistress, I don't know. She had a queer sort of code. She never forgot an injury or a kindness, and Ava had been very kind to her. I like to think that would have restrained Bess from taking Jerome as her lover, though most people thought differently.

"I met them once, walking on Cobbledick Hill, and I must admit there was something . . . kindred spirits, a oneness of mind . . . one could not deny it.

"That was a very cold year, I remember. The river was swollen, the ponds froze over. The Campions held a great Christmas Ball at Amberside, to which I was invited . . . the last ball ever, as it turned out.

"How splendid it looked, the rooms decked out in greenery and Christmas baubles, the ballroom throbbing with light and sound, Ava and Jerome standing at the head of the stairway to receive. It was the build-up to those parties that made them so exciting, you know. We have nothing like it now.

"One could see at once that Ava was far from well. Jerome told me quietly that she had had one of her attacks that morning and should not be up at all, but she had insisted.

"One of the first people I met was Bess. She looked very striking, in an ivory silk dress trimmed with ecru, and a string of pearls that was undoubtedly real. She was a big woman, you know, with glorious bold eyes and a manner of speech that was unconsciously dramatic. One felt her vitality and ambition, and one also felt, somehow, that she matched Amberside. She had a voluptuous intelligence that would have appealed to the architects and decorators of the eighteenth century.

"She saw me gazing at the pearls, and she smiled. 'Ava gave them to me. Aren't they beautiful?'

" 'Very. But are they wise?'

" 'Who cares about wisdom?' she said. That might have been her motto.

"The gathering that night was of particular interest to

me, composed as it was of people of influence. As the crowds filled the rooms, I lost sight of Bess. I left at two o'clock in the morning.

"A few hours later I was woken by my mother, who gave me the sad news. Ava Campion was dead. Her maid had taken in her breakfast tray, and found her lying dead on the floor of her bedroom. Apparently she had suffered some sort of seizure during the night, had started to get out of bed, and had collapsed and died almost immediately."

XVIII

Randall Jecks stopped speaking and fell into an abstracted silence as if his own story had made him forget Margot's presence. He shook his head.

"It was all very terrible...."

"And Bess Tuckett? She was suspected of poisoning Mrs Campion?"

"Oh no, no." Randall sounded horrified. "Nothing of the sort. Dr Wolpert was summoned and there was another house-guest, a Dr Roberts from London. Both of them knew that Ava had been in frail health for years. They found she had died of a very severe attack of cardiac asthma, which had led to heart failure.'

"Why had she got out of bed, though?"

"To fetch medicine, perhaps ... open a window ... in such an attack the patient can't get her breath, you see."

"Then why the suggestion of poison, later? And what sort of poison?"

"Digitalis. Mrs Campion was on a daily regimen of digitalis pills. The drug is obtained from the common foxglove, you know."

"But no one could confuse such a primitive concoction with pills put up by a chemist...."

"Of course not." Jecks held up a little white hand. "But let me tell it as it happened."

95

He leaned back in his chair once more. "There was no talk of poisoning, or any such nonsense, at first. I attended Ava's funeral like a good many other people. It was a fine service. Dr Mason of St Swithin's came down to play the organ, and there was some splendid singing from the choir and congregation. It must have pleased dear Ava." Opaque eyes fastened on Margot. "Do you believe in the after-life, Dr Wootten? Do you accept that those who pass over are close to us, watching us, hearing us... ?"

Margot said nothing, and Jecks continued. "The interment was the more melancholy for being effected the day before Christmas. It cast a gloom over the whole of the festive season."

"According to Ned Rubidge, there was a graveside scene."

"Quite untrue. In those days, people of good standing did not make scenes in public."

"Was there any feeling at Amberside, against Bess?"

"None whatsoever. She had been close to Ava, and felt her loss most grievously."

"Did she show it?"

"In her own fashion. Not by tears. Bess wasn't the sort to weep. But one could see she suffered."

"And Jerome?"

"He was shattered. He loved his wife."

"As well as loving Bess?"

"Can you not envisage such a case?"

"Yes. I can. So, when did the rumours start?"

"Months later. In June, during the period of intensive work for the Amber Festival. Jerome Campion had given me a job. I was integrating the programme for publication, dealing with the correspondence from a number of artists and ensembles, and so on. Jerome of course was in command of the whole thing, he had a great administrative gift. He had chosen the theme of romantic music for the first week, and moderns for the second. In this second part, he was anxious to present something British. One evening, I was summoned to dinner at Amberside. It was not a formal affair—Jerome, his son Richard and Ianthe, who was now Richard's wife, and myself were the only people present.

"Jerome waited until after we had dined, and then, when we were sitting in the music-room, he handed me a folder. It contained a number of poems, written in his own hand.

" 'Read them,' he said. 'Read them aloud.' "

"I did so. They formed a cycle, a story of rustic love, found and then lost—hardly an original theme, but the poetry had merit. It was intensely felt, and expressive, and it had been written, I was sure, by a man who had music in mind as he wrote.

" 'They would be better still set to music,' I told him. I half hoped, even then, that he would give me the task of providing that music. Jerome gave me a conspiratorial smile.

" 'That is the advantage of being an impresario,' he said. 'One can foist one's own work upon a helpless public, eh, Randall?'

"I felt jubilant. But before more could be said, Ianthe burst out, 'But Father, you simply can't do it.'

"Jerome looked surprised. 'Who is to stop me?'

"I've said Ianthe was a prude, but on this occasion her anger carried away her inhibitions. She stood up. Her face was pale. 'If you publish those poems, everyone will know they were written about Bess Tuckett.'

"It was a most improper thing to say, but it had the brute force of truth. However, Jerome's temper flared. 'I don't give a damn for small-minded gossip,' he said. 'I leave that to vulgarians.'

"Dicky Campion intervened. 'Ianthe's right, you know,

97

Father. People have malicious tongues, and you could make things very hard for Bess.'

"That made Jerome stop and think, and he put the poems aside and we got down to discussing the Festival. But that small incident made me realise how deeply he felt about Bess, and I knew that sooner or later we should have to face the fact. He was free to marry if he wished, and though Bess was hardly his equal by the standards of the time, she came of vigorous, talented stock.

"As it turned out, it was Bess's own temperament that brought about a crisis. If she had been content to wait a year or two, and keep her head and her temper, no doubt she and Jerome would have overcome the opposition to the match. But she was neither patient, nor calm. She was lonely, she was in love, she had never tolerated criticism, and she was extremely ambitious.

"Jerome decided to make Bess the innovation of the 1913 Festival. He planned to give her her first concert platform as a Lieder-singer, and he did her the honour of billing her, in the advance notices, with some of Europe's finest artists. It was not, in musical terms, a great risk to take. Bess had a truly lovely voice, and none of us doubted she had a future; but she should have been presented on lesser platforms first. Also, by choosing her, Jerome offended other local artists.

"From the time the programme was made public, in late July, jealousy was rampant in Amber. There was a pro-Bess and an anti-Bess faction. The antis didn't hesitate to smear her reputation, and these tales got back to her. She responded by attacking her enemies, and adopting a very arrogant manner.

"The highlight of the romantic section of the Festival was to be a presentation of the opera *Cinderella*. You know it? The lead rôle demands special qualities of the voice, great range, flexibility, warmth. The diva of the visiting company had such a voice, but in appearance, alas, she was a disaster. Squat, fat, forty and plain.

"Bess was heard to remark, at a rehearsal, that 'the poor old duck would be better as an ugly sister'. At once, one of her rivals took her up.

" 'I suppose you'd like to be Cinderella?'

" 'Not I,' said Bess. 'My feet are too big.'

" 'Ah, but you'd like to marry the handsome prince, wouldn't you?'

"So the fat was in the fire. The rehearsal became a slanging match, and it wasn't just over Bess, but involved the opera company as well. Jerome had to step in. To stop any further trouble, he made two things plain. Firstly, Bess must apologise for insulting the diva. Secondly, he intended to marry Bess in the spring of the following year.

"You can imagine that this merely exacerbated feelings. Not only was Bess being given the Festival plum, she was to have Jerome and Amberside as well. Added to jealousy, was the distaste that the engagement came so soon after the death of Ava. It was soon after this that one began to hear murmurs that Ava's dying had cleared the way for Bess, and that perhaps there was more to it than one knew.

"It was only vague hints, at first. This one said Ava would have rung for help if she'd been suffering an attack, not climbed out of bed. That one pointed out that as Ava was used to swallowing draughts made up by Bess, it would be easy to slip digitalis or some other poison into one of them. Soon there was a story that someone had 'gone to the police', and that the family wanted to 'have the body up'. The police denied they had been approached, the family was horrified at any idea of exhumation. Dr Wolpert said repeatedly that the death of Ava was from natural causes, he had signed the certificate because he was entirely satisfied, and it was rubbish to suggest that Mrs Campion died from an overdose of digitalis, that it was lack of stimulation, rather, that had caused her heart to fail. Instead of calming suspicion, this simply led to more rumours about mysterious poisons that only Bess knew about. It was all very wicked and very horrible, and it caused great suffering to many people, particularly Bess and Jerome.

"This talk ran on for four months. Bess never lost her courage, but the effect on her was dreadful. She came to mistrust even her friends. She avoided people, and spent most of her time alone, out at the farm, or walking on Cobbledick Hill. When one met her, she looked drawn and haunted. But she would not withdraw from the Festival.

"The climax came at the very concert Jerome had planned to honour Bess. It was held in the Wool Hall. I could not attend, as I was confined to my room, recovering from a virulent attack of influenza. But of course there were many witnesses to what happened.

"There was a packed audience, visiting and local people. At first things went smoothly. Bess sang her opening songs very well. Then suddenly, a faction of villagers at the back of the hall began to boo and hiss. They threw garbage at the stage, and shouted 'whore' and 'murderess'. Scuffles broke out, and the police were called, and then in an onset of madness some of the men rushed the stage. Jerome hustled Bess away, and turned to run down the curtain. The concert was over, the hall cleared.

"One can only guess what happened after. Bess was frantic with distress. She must have run from the building. Apparently Jerome followed her. The river was in full flood. Bess took the path along it. Either she threw herself into the water, or slipped and fell in, and Jerome must have tried to save her. They both lost their lives."

XIX

AT THIS POINT, Randall Jecks once more broke off his story, and directed a look of some shrewdness at his guest.

"A tragic end to a sad situation. But you can rest assured, Dr Wootten, that there was no element of crime in any of these events."

"Then, why the tombstone?"

"I know nothing of that." Margot was certain he was lying. There was a slyness in his manner. He had regained his poise, and she knew it would be of no use to pursue the matter, but his evasiveness interested her. She changed her line.

"Did you set Jerome's lyrics to music after his death?"

"Yes, the orchestration was completed that very month. A final . . . ah . . . tribute to his honourable work for music. His son gave me permission, naturally."

"A tribute to Jerome and to Bess, I'd say."

"What do you mean?"

"She inspired the poems. She would presumably have sung them. The woman's part is for a voice of extraordinary range . . . a voice like hers."

"Possibly she inspired Jerome. She did not inspire me." Jecks sounded both tired and waspish. He had become once more the pompous little dictator of the choir rehearsal. "I'm afraid my dear young lady, that I have work that must be done. . . ."

"Of course. I'm sorry to have taken so much of your time. If I may ask one or two quick questions . . . ?"

Jecks spread his hands.

"You mentioned Mrs Ianthe Campion, and the thought came to me that she might have records of the Festival . . . ?"

"She has."

"Where are they housed? At Amberside?"

"No. That is closed. Jerome's death in 1913, and Dicky's in France two years later, brought such large death duties that it couldn't be fully maintained. It's suffered a chequered career. Ianthe moved out during the Second World War, settled in the Dower House, just across the river. The old tithe barn next to it has been turned into the Barn Museum, and contains all the relics of the Festival, going back over a brace of centuries."

"Could I see over it?"

"You would need to ask the Campions' permission. It's closed at this time of the year, and Ianthe is rather a stickler for protocol. Still, you could try."

"I will." Margot rose, so did her host. As he walked to the door with her, Margot glanced out of the window. "Is it possible to walk along the river bank and reach the inn?"

"Yes, but take care. The tow-path is nearly awash."

He opened a french window on to the lawn, and pointed to where a line of willows masked a causeway. Across the river she could see steep slopes, clothed with woods. Above these, the sky was sombre. The air struck cold, and her companion shivered.

"That's Ianthe's property," he said. "Up there, on the right, you see the roofs? The barn is the larger, the Dower House behind it."

Margot said goodbye and set out along the path. It was treacherous in parts, with tracts of glassy mud sloping to the water. A couple more inches, and the flood would cover it. Willows trailed their fronds. In November, when Bess Tuckett died, they would have been pollarded. Nothing to catch hold of.

She walked on slowly. To the left, beyond the copse, rose the tower of St Ringan's and the bulk of the Wool Hall. Ahead and far away, the upper storey of Amberside. And across the water, the woods, tangled fern and bracken, dead trees aslant among the living. Strange that they should be neglected in a farming area like this.

There was more rain coming. The temperature was dropping steadily.

She reached the ford, wider than it had been the previous night, and topped by a curdled brown foam. As she watched, a white branch swept under the bridge and tossed past her. She remembered her dream of drowning ... her sense of rage and fear. Perhaps it was her own anger that had expressed itself through the half-world of sleep. Perhaps it was the older anger of Bess Tuckett.

She stood still, trying to envisage what must have happened. There would have been the turmoil in the concert hall, the shouting, the confusion, the accusations of adultery and murder. Bess must have run from some back door, into the darkness. Had she really thrown herself into the water? Wasn't it more likely that she'd slipped on the tow-path, and plunged in? She was not the sort to take her own life. The demon that possessed Amber was fury, not despair.

Another possibility occurred to her. Jerome Campion had followed Bess to the river. He loved the woman who was suspected of poisoning his wife. His position must have been ugly, even if he believed her innocent. What if, that last night, he had come to think her guilty?

What had happened in this place?

As she stood deliberating, someone ran from the woods above the ford, crossed over the bridge, saw her and halted. Blue jeans and a cocksure stance identified Chilli Gold. He raised a hand and waved.

"Hi," he said as she approached. "What are you doing here?"

"That's my line," she said. "I called on Randall Jecks."

"Oh? And what did you think of him?"

"He talked a lot."

"And?"

"There's something a bit camp about him, but he's no fool." Margot glanced skyward as a flurry of rain struck them. "He told me Ava Campion died of natural causes, no doubt of it."

"Well," said Chilli, "so will we if we stand about here. Come to The Ram, and I'll give you lunch."

XX

THEY WERE THE only people in the dining-room. Mrs Rubidge served them herself. She looked harassed, and Margot wondered if she had heard about the quarrel between Will Asher and Niall Campion. If so, she did not mention it.

Chilli, on the other hand, was talkative. He asked a number of questions about her talk with Randall Jecks. After a while he said bluntly:

"Margot, haven't you asked yourself why you let Bess Tuckett bug you?"

"I think it's a sort of fellow feeling."

"Yes, but why?"

"Do I have to give reasons to anyone?"

"To yourself, maybe."

She shrugged. This response seemed to anger him. "You drive in here like a crazy woman, don't know what you're doing, where you're going. You're touchy as hell and you slap down anyone who tries to question you. In my book, people who behave like you are yelling for help."

"I am not. I specifically don't want pity, I don't want advice, I don't want interference of any sort. Is that clear?"

"Clear. I hear you. So I'll drop any idea of helping you to fix an appointment with Ianthe Campion."

"Who said I wanted one?"

"Oh, grow up!"

There was pause. Then she said, "I shall simply ask her."

"You won't get far. She's very old, and dislikes strangers."

"Could you fix it?"

"Perhaps."

"Why you?"

He gave his three-cornered smile. "Call it business interests."

"Then, please would you try?"

"Sure."

When the meal was over, he went out into the hall, where he made a lengthy telephone call. Coming back to her, he told her that Mrs Ianthe Campion would be pleased to see Dr Wootten at the Dower House, at three o'clock.

XXI

By a quarter to three the showers seemed to have stopped. Margot, armed with Chilli's directions, drove across the bridge, and took the narrow road that forked right from the main highway, then right again.

Amberside now lay behind her. The track led upwards through encroaching woods to a pair of gates, standing open. She drove through, rounded a shoulder of land and emerged suddenly in a wide clearing.

On her right, the steep fall of ground had been shorn to afford a view of the river. Directly ahead was a massive building with a shingled roof. This she took to be the tithe barn, now a museum. Its walls had been pierced by doors and windows, and there was flat parking-ground beyond it.

Further to the left stood the Dower House, L-shaped, a pleasant structure of brick and clapboard, joined to the barn by an enclosed passageway of much more recent date.

Margot parked the Fiat in a corner between house and passage, and picked her way over puddles of rainwater to the front door. A wistaria vine dripped water on to her shoulders. Mud clung to the footscraper by the step, and the brass knocker was green with verdigris.

Her knock brought the sound of brisk footsteps, and the door swung inward. The man standing there must, she knew, be in his late fifties, no, sixty; but he looked younger. Not a grey hair in the beautifully cut, longish hair. No fat at the waistline. He wore country clothes of the trendy, expensive sort. In the gloom of the entrance she could not see his face clearly.

"Dr Wootten?" She recognised the fluting tones from Will Asher's garage. "I'm Niall Campion. Please come in."

He did not offer her his hand but closed the door after her and stood looking at her for a moment.

"Don't I know you from somewhere?"

"I don't think we've met."

"Your name is familiar."

She gave him a vague smile. He seemed about to press the question, but changed his mind and led the way through the house to a small sitting-room.

"My mother has been resting. I'll go and fetch her now, if you wouldn't mind waiting."

He went off. Margot moved to the window. The sky was lighter over the autumnal woods, and she looked straight down the hill, to the raging Amber river, and on the far side, the graceful houses of Ringan's Close. It seemed that the Campions, as a family, liked a wide prospect. Strange, how looking from a height gave one the illusion of superiority over what lay below. I'm the king of the castle, and you're the dirty rascal.

The room was a retreat typical of its kind; the stronghold of an old and wealthy woman, strewn with tokens of prestige, sentiment and achievement. Margot studied a phalanx of photographs. Some lovely soft sepia prints of Edwardian children; belles in boas and huge hats; an assortment of Lenares and Beatons from the 1930s. Place of honour went to a fair man in the uniform of World War One, probably the defunct Dicky Campion.

Chairs, recently upholstered in antiqued velvet; desk open to show neat stacks of letters and bills; a new novel, in the large-print edition, open on the sofa. A smell of lemon verbena and money, discreetly applied. Margot turned back to face the door.

The Campions entered together. They were much of a height, and looked alike, oval-faced, straight-nosed, small-mouthed. While there might not be much affection between them, there seemed to be perfect understanding.

"Dr Wootten, I hope Niall apologised for me? I'm afraid I fell asleep after luncheon."

Her voice was like her son's, light yet measured, intended to charm even while it held at a distance. Margot found herself thinking of the ritual greetings of primitive people, who use these forms to give warning of their purpose, war or peace.

Frail fingers brushed hers, indicated a chair, lifted to tug a Dior jacket into place.

"Such miserable weather. Niall, are we warm enough in here? Perhaps if you would turn that object up a notch? That's it, thank you." Her eyes, huge, blue and sunken under the delicate lids of old age, glanced with dissatisfaction at the electric heater. "I prefer a fire," she said.

"No one will clean grates nowadays, Mother."

"I can't think why not. We pay them enough."

Niall Campion sat down opposite Margot. "I'm afraid we don't know quite what you want of us, Dr Wootten. You're a friend of Chilli Gold, I gather?"

"Not really. I'm in Amber by chance. My car ran out of petrol and Mr Gold rescued me. I booked in at The Ram, attended a choir practice because I like choral music, and heard about your Festival museum. I hoped to visit it."

"Unfortunately it's closed at this time of year. We have to keep to the rules, or the custodian would never get his leave. I expect Randall did mention that to you."

"Yes." So Randall had lost no time in reporting her visit to his friends.

"Is there some question we could answer, perhaps?"

109

"I'm interested in the Campion songs."

Ianthe gave a faint sigh, which might indicate boredom or regret.

"I fear," said Niall, "we're not much help. I have no time for music, and my mother is tone deaf."

"I don't mean the music, but the poems ... that your grandfather wrote. There's something unusual about them. They are very modern in form. I'd like to see the original text."

"You're a doctor of literature, are you?"

"No. Are the originals of the poems in the museum?"

"I believe they are. As I remember, one can hardly decipher them. Jerome Campion wrote an atrocious hand. What exactly is it that you're looking for?"

"I'm not sure I know. In any case, if the museum is closed ..."

He interrupted her. "You met Gold for the first time, here in Amber?"

"Yes."

"A talented young man. I've known him for years. I suppose the life of the pop guitarist is conducive to trouble-making."

"He said he was quitting that scene."

Niall nodded abstractedly, as if he was weighing some consideration in his own mind. Finally he straightened.

"Let me be frank. I'm an industrialist ..." His mother made a slight sound of mockery, at which her son's face coloured. "An industrialist, not a jaded aristo. I have factories all over the home counties, they employ a lot of people and contribute handsomely to the economy. I'm neither musical nor an intellectual, but one thing I know damn well, and that's what will happen to Britain if we can't pull out of the inflationary spin. One way to do that is to increase the number of factories in useless land like ours—and factories nowadays are not the reeking mills of

110

yesteryear, Mother, whatever you may think. I want to tell you, Dr Wootten, that I can't stomach the sort of treacly sentiment that passes for thought among my opponents here."

"What do they want?"

"They want to live in the past. Revive a festival that was never economically viable and would be less so today. They want to keep bricks and stones intact when they should be thinking about jobs and productivity."

"And profits?"

"And profits, of course." He offered her a cigarette, lit one himself, and eyed her through a haze of smoke. "Do you object to that?"

"No."

"Tax takes it all," said Ianthe Campion, "and what is left, buys nothing. Trashy stuff. I don't know why you waste your time, Niall, bothering about people. . . ."

"What people?" demanded her son impatiently.

She turned her head towards the window, with its view of the village. "Why do you argue with them? I would go straight to the Minister."

Margot broke in on this train of thought. "I really don't know anything about East Amber, or industry. But I do know you have a fine choir here, that can sing the Campion songs as they should be sung . . . with lute accompaniment."

At that, Niall rose suddenly, stubbing out his cigarette. "I believe, Dr Wootten, that we should make an exception for you, and show you the museum. It's nothing great, understand. Mother, have you the key?"

Mrs Campion nodded. She rose and crossed to the desk, found the key and brought it back to her son, dropping it into his hand with a gesture that said, "Well, if you must. . . ." She must have been beautiful in youth, though Margot doubted if those large blue eyes had ever seen a joke. Was she intelligent? Stupid? One couldn't know. She had lived over eighty years, most of them as a widow. A lifetime of loneliness . . . or not?

They walked to the barn through the connecting passage. Niall kept at Margot's side, his mother drifted along behind them. There were some beautiful pictures on the walls, landscapes, no portraits, and at the first corner, a ledge held a little clock of Sèvres porcelain.

Niall unlocked double doors and threw them open. The barn was a splendid old building, whose lofty timbered roof was now partly obscured by modern ceilings. The air was surprisingly warm. There were central heating pipes at intervals along the walls. At the near end, a number of chairs had been ranged round two low tables, to make a reading area. Beyond were the glass cases, felt-covered stands and printed notices common to all museums.

Ianthe Campion did not accompany them on their tour, but sat down in one of the easy chairs, leaning back in it with closed eyes. Her hands drooped over the armrests. How tiresome, her posture said, how dreary all this is!

Niall conducted Margot from case to case. The exhibits had the slightly musty bloom of objects that are kept clean, but never used. She gazed at sheafs of music, handcarved instruments, theatrical costumes; at designs for sets, and plans for the modernisation of the Wool Hall. A bad painting showed ranks of dignitaries at the official opening. Jerome Campion stood at centre, bearded and correct. The thin little woman clinging to his arm must be Ava.

At last they came to the book in which Jerome had written his poems. It was open at the first lyric of the Campion Cycle.

"Would you like to handle it?" asked Niall.

"Very much."

He unlocked the case and lifted out the book, beautiful as books had been at that time, with soft suede covers and pages of thick vellum, edged with gold. Jerome's writing was slanting and vigorous. The poems had no titles, only numbers, and each was signed individually. A curious touch, that, as if the writer was attesting the depth of his commitment to love, for future readers to see.

The irregular form, which she had noticed in the printed folio, was even more noticeable here. Some lines were only one or two words long, others ran for several phrases. A style completely individual.

The form, the content, the writing expressed erotic love. Margot glanced at Ianthe in her chair. No wonder the lyrics had offended her. They were not meant to placate. They had been written to throw in the world's face.

She replaced the book in its case. Next to it lay a sheaf of manuscript music, the score for the Cycle. Signed, though not in defiance, by Randall Jecks, it contained no lute part.

She moved on. Niall produced at her request a bundle of old Festival programmes. She leafed through them to find the one she wanted. Bess Tuckett's name was on the cover, as soloist. She had engaged to sing two Schubert Lieder, two Brahms, some unaccompanied songs (anonymous), an aria from Carmen and one from La Traviata. The choice of music was in itself a description of the woman, as well as of her voice.

Margot laid the programmes aside with a feeling of pity. They walked back towards the main door. Almost the last thing they passed was a little table draped in dark blue velvet, on which rested a fiddle, a bow, a flute and a lute. Niall smiled. "There's schmaltz for you."

"Your grandfather's?" Margot bent to examine the lute, which was in good condition, the decoration of painted flowers discernible round the throat.

"So the catalogue says. I'm afraid they're being reprinted, or I'd give you one. Yes, this little lot belonged to the old boy."

"They weren't meant for silence."

"What?"

"They should be played. They're good. This," she touched the lute, "is old, very old. It's been repaired. here, you see? This strip of wood in the belly is newer, though it's beautifully matched. Perhaps the work was done in Amber."

"Most likely. Grandfather was a great one for supporting the local craftsmen."

"Is there a portait of him, or his wife?"

"Nothing worth looking at. They were both done, of course, by Sickert and others, but all those went to his sister's branch of the family, whom we don't ever see. I think there were some albums of photos, when I was a boy, but they had nothing to do with the Festival. I expect they've been thrown out by now."

"Impossible people," said Ianthe, opening her eyes with the sudden alertness of the light sleeper. Then, as Margot and Niall turned to look at her, she rose from her chair and headed for the door. They saw her walk along the corridor and vanish round the corner without a backward glance.

"At eighty-three," said Niall, "my mother is an erratic hostess. She doesn't mean to be rude."

He took Margot back to the front door. There was no sign of Mrs Campion. "Well, Dr Wootten, I hope your curiosity is assuaged."

"You've been very helpful."

"Tell me." He contemplated her with a half smile. "You spoke to Randall about Bess Tuckett. I half suspected you were from the press, looking for old scandals."

"No."

"I'm glad to hear it. It would be distressing for my mother. She had her fill of it."

He led her to her car, opened the door for her. The rain had cleared entirely now, and the clouds rested as lightly as bubbles on Cobbledick Hill.

As Margot started the car, Niall bent suddenly to the window.

"Wootten," he said. "I've remembered. You were on the Shapiro expedition to the Amazon, weren't yo", with your husband? Read about him in the press. He spoke at some society, done great work, something like that?"

Margot turned the ignition key. The engine kicked. Niall grinned and moved back, hand uplifted.

She swung the Fiat out of the yard and down the track through the woods. As it emerged on to the main road, she saw Chilli Gold perched on the parapet of the bridge. He sprang down, signalling her to stop.

"Hi." He slid into the passenger seat before she could stop him. "Been waiting for you, over an hour. Someone phoned for you. A Dr Seuffert. Very anxious to talk to you, Nancy Rubidge said."

Margot jerked round to face him.

"I checked the number," he went on. "Seuffert is the psychiatrist at the Lovell Clinic for Neuro-diseases in Birmingham. Is that what you're running away from, love?"

His eyes, golden in the fading light, had the menace and mockery of Pan. Symbolically, she felt the onset of panic, fear.

"How dare you spy on me?"

"Not spying." His fingers slowly brushed her arm. "I'm as crazy as you are. But what about this doc?"

She forced herself to a semblance of calm. "I will phone him tonight."

"Now," Chilli told her. "Better do it now, because something tells me that if you don't, he's going to set the police and God knows who else after you."

115

XXII

S HE LET CHILLI GOLD stand at her side while she spoke to the Lovell Clinic people. It took them a while to find Dr Seuffert, five-thirty being the time he took a break between hospital rounds, and his group therapy class.

Eventually a tired voice said, "Hello."

"It's me. Margot Wootten."

"About time. Are you speaking from The Ram?"

"Yes."

"We've been worried about you."

She said nothing, frowning at the carved panel behind the phone. She heard him sigh.

"You always reduce me to ridiculous remarks like that one. I'm actually in need of your help. Do you know where Patrick is?"

"Patrick who?"

"Your ex-husband, Patrick Wootten, has disappeared. The girl, Vivien what's-her-name, was admitted to the General Hospital late on Friday, and had the child. It was a breech birth and she damn near died. She's been calling for Patrick and he's nowhere to be found. . . ."

Margot laughed softly. "You're lying, Doc. You panicked, didn't you? You phoned all the hospitals, and they told you at the General I'd been admitted. Only it turned out not to be me, but Vivien. And then the hospital desk told you another Mrs Wootten had called, from Amber. I'm not coming back, you know."

"Margot . . ."

"I am not coming back. Understand?"

"I understand. To return to my question, do you know where Patrick is?"

"Why the hell should I? I haven't seen him for months."

"The girl is really very ill."

"Oh, my Christ!" She turned and leaned her back against the wall and closed her eyes. She remembered lying in that spinning place where fever was her sole companion, those monstrous dreams and the waking worse, she remembered how she'd screamed for Patrick. What had they told her? Idiocies. "Listen," she told the receiver. "Listen carefully. What do I care for the girl or him? I've told you. Haven't I? And you can . . ."

A thought struck her and she fell silent. Her forefinger reached up to twist a strand of her hair. She could not say what she wanted to, but she had forgotten Seuffert's acute perceptions.

"The child is all right. It's a girl," he said, and then waited patiently while she let that answer sink into her. At last, "Margot?"

"Yes."

"Have you really no idea where he is?"

"I . . . I don't know . . ."

"Try and think."

"His mother."

"Where?"

"She's . . . twenty-three, Lincoln Road, Luton."

"Thank you, Margot. And look after yourself. Hear me?"

She dropped the receiver on to the cradle. She could feel the muscles of her face and throat contracting towards

117

hysteria and this time she couldn't fight it. Tears began to stream down her cheeks. She lifted her arms, and Chilli caught hold of her, hustled her across the hallway and up to the shelter of her room.

XXIII

IT WAS CHILLI who nursed her through the storm, battling her as she struck out at him, and later helping her to undress, tucking the blankets round her, talking to her in the matter-of-fact voice one uses to a querulous child.

At one point, incensed by his very calm, she railed at him and called him a fraud. He paused in the task of picking up the clothes she'd tossed to the floor.

"Why fraud?"

"You're phoney. You don't fool me."

He said mildly, "I never tried to. I'd have liked to talk, but you don't encourage confidences." He came across and sat on the edge of the bed. "Here's one. Most of the time I don't see things very clearly. Play it by ear, no sight-reading. But sometimes, things seem to come into focus. It may be I'm on my own, or with another person. It can happen anywhere. But I feel whole, you know? I am aware. Past, present and future, it's all one and I understand, not just by thinking but like with the whole of myself. And that's living. Have you ever felt like that? And another thing, I believe it's the present that explains the past, not the other way about. Now I'm here, with you, I can understand a lot of things that happened to me before. Now I'd like you to think about that and give me an explanation, one day."

"You're just talking," she said. A drowiness was engulfing her, she was a ship tossing on a dark sea... rocking... why would he want to come with her on such a journey?

"Go to sleep," he was saying.

" 'A lifetime burning in every moment'," she murmured. "That's what you mean."

"Yes. That's it. Go to sleep."

This time, she obeyed him.

She woke before it was light. The curtains were blowing on a steady breeze, and the inner sill of the window was wet.

She lay for some time, thinking, and then got up and bathed and dressed. She threw her belongings into her case and shut it, put on her coat and went quietly downstairs. The young girl was at the desk. Margot settled her account, got the Fiat out of the garage, and gave the key to a man cleaning the yard.

The main street was deserted, but as she drove past St Ringan's she saw the lights were on in the main porch. She parked the car and walked across the turf to the graveyard, making her way for the second time to Bess Tuckett's grave. She stared at it, bent down and thrust her hand into the tufts of long grass at its foot, so that beads of rainwater soaked her sleeve.

The present explains the past, not the other way about. East Amber now explains East Amber then. I explain Bess Tuckett.

She went into the church.

Coker Brown was moving about above the chancel steps, and one or two other people. In the nimbus of light up there they looked warm and secure.

Margot walked round the nave.

No lights here, air dim and cold, but not unwelcoming.

She was aware of numberless people long dead and yet to be born, who pressed between the smooth black columns.

The Campions were buried in stone instead of earth. Here they lay, crusaders in long-toed splendour, ladies broken-nosed and lily-handed, children in marble petti-coats. She moved along the line. Thomas Campion, one of the most remote, seemed a contemporary. His face in its encircling helmet had defied the carver's efforts at solemnity. If one touched his shoulder he would spring up with an oath and a jest. Here was Jerome Campion, cast in bronze, wearing the same look of arrogant ribaldry. (Why does it seem familiar? I have not been here before.) Many of the tombs bore the token campion flower.

She was near the chancel now. Beyond the screen, she could see old Ned Rubidge, setting out prayer books in the choir stalls. He looked all of his seventy-eight years this morning. His shoulders were hunched, his face grey and he had the shakes. When he caught sight of Margot he stopped in his tracks and then started to shuffle away along the pew. On impulse, she ran up to the far end, cutting off his retreat.

"Good morning, Mr Rubidge."

"Mornin'."

"Do you know where Mr Brown is?"

"Vestry I s'pose."

"I've come to say goodbye."

"Leavin', are yer? That's right. Leave 'er be, I say. Don't meddle with the dead."

"I wonder, is Bess Tuckett really dead?"

"'Course she is, deader'n a doorstop. Anyone says otherwise is a wicked sinner, like she was."

"Let him that is without sin cast the first stone."

The old man turned scarlet. He raised his fist. "I never cast no stone, and don't you say so!"

Before Margot could respond, a step sounded and she

121

saw Coker Brown coming towards her. Rubidge muttered something and made for the far aisle.

"Hello, Margot. I saw you out there in the gloom. Come over to the house and have breakfast with us."

"Thanks, Coker, but I'm just leaving."

"Oh?" He looked startled and a little hurt, but recovered quickly. "Does Chilli know?"

"Will you tell him for me?"

"If you wish. Will you be coming back?"

"No."

He stared at her intently. "You are looking better, yes, but still not well. Take care of yourself. If you change your mind and want some country air, we can always offer you a bed. Remember?"

"I will. You've been very kind, all of you." She put out her hand and felt it warmly clasped. "Give Zillah my love."

He nodded. Margot hurried away through the lightening church, out into the roadway. The sun was up.

By nine o'clock she was driving through the outskirts of London.

XXIV

SHE BOOKED INTO a small hotel in St John's Wood. She had made up her mind to forget East Amber, and the people she had met there. That done, she seemed incapable of further decisions.

She walked on Hampstead Heath, and rode sometimes on buses picked at random; went to a cinema and fell asleep, seeing nothing but the credits; ate alone in the most crowded places possible.

At night she suffered from recurrent nightmares, in which the terror took the form of an inexorable companion, never seen, but known. Sometimes she lolled on a tropical sea, knowing that its miasma hid another swimmer. Sometimes it was a footfall that betrayed the presence, and sometimes the intensity of a silence.

One night as she reached for her bottle of capsules, she caught sight of her reflection in the looking-glass. The outstretched hand was not her own, but the hand of Bess Tuckett. She swung round to face the empty room.

"Let me be. You're none of my business."

The unseen shadow answered; in the present the past is explained, in my life, your life. You can't deny yourself.

On Friday she went to see the man who had been—still was—her employer. The Kirkwood Institute was in Middlesex, its function the promotion of ecological research. Owen Hood, its director, sat fractious behind a stack of reports; his little bear's eyes glinted at her, half pleased and half wary.

"Well, woman, how are you?"

"Better." She took the chair facing him. "I'd like to start work next month."

"Good. Got clearance from the quacks?"

"I don't need anyone's permission. I told you."

He grunted. "So did they, as it happens. You didn't have to run out on them, Margot. It upset them."

She moved her shoulders impatiently and he frowned.

"You're a self-centred and stubborn bitch, know that? Can't you understand that people care what happens to you?"

"Because I might do something awkward if they don't keep an eye on me!"

"No. Because they are fond of you, God knows why, and because you happen to be one of the more useful of the younger scientists in your field. Food, good wench, is the concern of anyone who gives a bugger about the future of mankind—and you are engaged in research into food resources. Nobody has to tell your doctors that we need you. They can read—the easy words, anyway—and that much of the truth has sunk home to them."

She turned her head aside. Then, "Is the book out yet?" As he made no answer: "Well, is it?"

He reached into a drawer and pulled out a volume, new, smelling of the press. He handed it to her. She looked at the spine. Patrick Wootten. She opened it. Facts, figures, drawings and photographs, most of them her own. She dropped the book on the desk.

"For Chrissake, Margot," said Owen, "why don't you sue him? You don't have to let him get away with it."

"We did the work together. Anyway, he hasn't got away with it."

"Umh?" Owen looked alarmed. "Have you seen him, then?"

"No. He phoned me, last Sunday week. He needed some answers. Seems that after he addressed the society, people started asking him to enlarge on the subject." She began to laugh quietly. Owen did not join in.

"And what did you say?"

"I told him to go look for the answers where I found them. In Xingu. That's a long way away."

"I know where it is," Owen said. He watched Margot with lowered chin. "Seuffert phoned me," he said. "Patrick's disappeared."

"When did you speak to Seuffert?"

"Yesterday . . . no, the day before. Do you know where the punk has gone?"

"No. Perhaps to Xingu. The girl had the baby, you know, so he's got that to run away from, too."

Owen sighed. "There was another enquiry about you."

"From?"

"A man I never heard of." Owen turned a memo-block towards him. "Chap called Niall Campion. Wanted to know about your Amazon trip, who was with you on the team, etcetera. Said he knew Mark Shapiro 'in his personal capacity'. I snubbed him."

"I don't think snubbing will put off Mr Campion. Tell me, what did you think was the real reason for his call? If he's not a botanist?"

"Thought he might be soft on you."

"The reverse, I'd say." She thought a little, then said, "He's an industrialist. Rich, greedy, wants to turn a nice little Suffolk village into a factory area."

"No law against that, is there?"

"None, except it would be poor ecology."

"You've been there?"

"Yes, it's a place called East Amber. The grasses are valuable, and intact. Flora diverse and rich."

"And campions everywhere, one gathers."

"Campions everywhere," she agreed. Suddenly she sat up straight. "In fact . . . you remind me . . ."

"Umh?"

"Of campions," she said. She got to her feet, gathering up coat and purse. "I must hurry."

"Where in God's name are you off to?"

"To a music agent," she told him, and headed for the door.

XXV

THE AGENCY OF Salmon and Massey was just off
Oxford Street. Margot chose it because she knew Jules
Salmon. He'd been a pupil of her father before going over
to the business side of music . . . and he was a know-all.
Information stuck to his mind like pollen to a pistil.

Margot found him spooning yoghurt from a plastic cup
and listening to a recording by Led Zeppelin. He switched
off the player and beckoned Margot in.

"How are you, darling? You look lovely."

"Fine."

Jules returned to earth. "No. Wait a minute, you're not,
are you? You went to some terrible place and caught a
dread disease?"

"I'm all right."

"And your husband walked out on you? Dunno who
told me. Is it true?"

"Yes. I didn't come to talk about that, Jules. Do you
know a guitarist called Chilli Gold?"

" 'Course. Good boy, the full cream, but he pulled out
last year."

"Why?"

"Dunno, couldn't say."

"What's his real name?"

"Chilli Gold."

127

"Nobody gets christened Chilli Gold."

"Well, that's his signature, darling, on the business documents. Really and truly."

"I see." She thought a while. "Do you know a song cycle by a man named Randall Jecks, lyrics by Jerome Campion?"

"Yeah, I heard it a couple of times."

"With lute accompaniment?"

"No, don't think so." He frowned, evidently listening to some inner playback. "Nope. But that might be nice, might be good."

"It is good, as played by Chilli Gold."

"I told you, the Jersey Cream is no fuller."

"Next question. Do you know Randall Jecks?"

"I met him once, twice."

"How do you rate him?"

"Musically, I don't. When he was impresario, he knew a lot of people, all the tricks. But he's the dodo, darling, doesn't rate nowadays."

"Rich?"

"Yes. His family was Jecks Jellies. Fact. The money helped to boost him, but he worked hard, I'm told. He was musician *manqué*, always wanted to make the concert platform but no real talent, so he did the next best thing, he promoted those who had it. Clap hands for Randall."

"When you said he knew all the tricks, you mean he was dishonest?"

"God, no. Slick, quick and a tough negotiator, you have to be to get good artists and terms. He had a solid reputation, no mistake. I met him once in Bayreuth. He knew all the opera buffs. Strutted among all those huge tenors and sopranos like a bantam in a flock of turkeys."

It was now close to noon. Margot thanked Jules, said goodbye and caught a bus to the Strand.

At Somerset House her search proved easier than she

128

had expected. She quickly found the birth certificates of Jerome Campion, and of his sister Helen. From there she moved to records of marriages, then back to births. By two o'clock she had what she wanted.

She borrowed a telephone directory from a friendly assistant, and looked up an address in Camden Hill; put through a call, found her quarry at home, and arranged an appointment. By two fifteen she had picked up her own car, and was heading west.

XXVI

"My father could not speak a word of English when he arrived in England. He was born in St Petersburg, and took part in the workers' march in 1905, Bloody Sunday you remember, when the Tsar's troops killed scores of marchers? He left Russia in 1906 and came to Paris, then London. A Russian teacher with no money, Orthodox Church views, Socialist leanings. Can you imagine anything less likely to attract the attention of an English county family?"

Margot smiled. She had liked her host on sight. He had the sort of long, thin face that expresses the lightest shade of emotion; rather prominent black eyes, sharp with humour; a very deep, soft voice. He was watching her with his head cocked to one side, as if she might supply the answer to an amusing riddle.

His house was an oddity. Outwardly a conventional Camden Hill three-storey, it had been radically altered within, to create large asymmetric living-rooms, galleries on two levels, and a spiral stairway at the core. All the furnishing and fitments were modern. There were several abstract paintings, a wall covered with blow-up photographs of buildings, a bay containing a bank of filing cabinets and calculating machines. "I am," the owner had explained, "an actuary who works at home."

"But your father," she now suggested, "did attract the Campions, so I suppose he had something going for him? Music, I'd say."

"Correct. He had two assets, a knowledge of French and a basso profundo voice. He joined a choir and found his way to the Amber Festival. Jerome Campion took him up and invited him to sing at one or two private concerts. Jerome's sister, my mother, fell in love with him. Since she was thirty-seven and regarded as eccentric, as well as having private means, she managed to fly in the face of opinion and marry my father. It was a very good marriage. I was the elder of two boys born to them. My parents settled in London, changing a difficult Russian surname to Gold. I was christened Achille John, the Achille for some remote Balkan forebear. My eldest son is Achille Hugh."

"Hence the Chilli?"

"Yes, a school nickname. It suited rather well when he was looking for something outlandish to please the pop world. He's made a success. Have you heard him play?"

"Not the guitar, but the lute—brilliantly."

Mr Gold looked complacent.

"What can you tell me," said Margot baldly, "about a woman called Bess Tuckett, who was drowned in the same accident as your uncle Jerome?"

"Practically nothing."

"I called on Mrs Ianthé Campion and her son. They told me that all the Campion portraits passed to your mother on Jerome's death."

"And you want to see them? Tell me, Mrs Wootten, your reason for digging up the past? It can be painful."

"An injustice was done."

His shrewd eyes considered her. "Not many people trouble their heads about injustice, unless they have a direct personal interest."

"I resent theft. There can be theft of reputation, of

131

credit. What if Bess Tuckett was innocent? She had no trial, no chance to defend herself. She's buried under a tombstone that condemns her as a woman who poisoned her friend and patron. That's how she'll go down in village legend."

"You think such things matter to the dead?"

"Does injustice cease to be injustice once the victim is dead? If so, why do we waste our time with trials and verdicts? We all die, so death will solve everything!"

His smile, gently ironical, galled her to anger. "All right, then, forget the dead. I'm concerned for the living. I was in Amber last week. You know what that place reeks of? Taboo, primitive taboo like you find among people without a culture. And do you know what's at the root of taboo? The taint of past crime or sin. You can smile, Mr Gold, but the villagers of Amber would not. They'd know what I'm talking about. If the word 'haunted' means anything, then Amber is haunted."

"By an unsolved crime?"

"By an unresolved guilt." She moved quickly towards him. "And I'll tell you something else. Chilli feels it. Twice, when I've been with him, I've known he feels it. It's not just my imagination."

"So Amber has a problem. It is their problem. Why should it concern you?" He leaned forward, pointing a finger. "What is your own interest in Bess Tuckett?"

"If I told you, you wouldn't understand."

"No? Then if I am so obtuse, there's no reason to prolong our discussion." He made as if to rise.

"Wait..."

"No, my dear. You demand confidences, but will give none in return. You come here with questions about a matter of the deepest concern to my family. You must validate your own motives before I answer those questions."

132

"Please, Mr Gold . . ."

"Very well, then. . . ." He settled back, signing to her to resume her seat. "You spoke of injustice. Have you yourself been a victim? And of what?"

Margot took time to gather her thoughts. Her host sat waiting, chin in hand.

"I am a botanist," she said at last. "Like my husband. We worked together, ten years dragging round the world. We couldn't have a home or children, we agreed on that, because the work we were doing was so important. It concerned global food supplies. When you make a great many sacrifices for an idea, then that idea can become obsessive. Patrick and I lost touch with reality, I guess. Other people didn't matter. Even when we were with a team, the two of us worked together all the time, shared every thought. We were preparing a book. It took us eight years to gather the material. It was going to be the definitive work, and more, it was going to be our house and children, it was going to make us famous and rich, and save the world from famine. It sounds ridiculous. . . ."

She looked at Gold, who shook his head silently.

"We were out in the Amazon basin," she went on, "at this place called Xingu, when Patrick's health failed. He was sent home early, almost a year before the rest of us.

"Just before the expedition was due to leave South America, I got typhus fever. It's a bad disease, affects the nervous system, gives you hallucinations. It can cause permanent brain damage. I was very ill. Even when the crisis was over, I was weak and couldn't sleep. I'd get these bouts of panic. They put me on a ship for England. All the way home I hung on to the thought that when I was with Patrick again, everything would be all right.

"He wasn't at Southampton to meet me. I went to the address I'd always written to, and he'd moved. I phoned his mother's home. She said she didn't know where he was.

133

She was lying. I suppose she was scared I'd harm him. She didn't know how sick I'd been, or she might have helped me. Anyway, it took me five days to trace Patrick and by that time I was nearly crazy. I traced him to Birmingham, eventually. When I found him, he had this girl with him. They'd rented a house.

"I can't tell you too much about what happened, what Patrick said. Just that he told me everything. The girl, the baby. He said we were finished, and he told me he'd taken the manuscript of the book to a publisher and it would be coming out soon, under his name only. It was as if he had to keep hitting me and hitting me with words. As if I was an insect he couldn't kill so he kept hitting. . . .

"I went back to the hotel where I'd booked in. Then I collapsed. They put me into the Lovell Clinic for Neuro-diseases. I was there for weeks, having treatment. I got over the fever itself, but I was in a terrible mess. I can't describe to you, to anyone, how I felt. I was like an empty house, breaking down, and the only thing that propped up the walls was hate. I hated Patrick like white fire. I spent every waking minute planning what I'd do. I took legal advice about how to bring an action against him, for publishing my work as his. I made up my mind I'd refuse him a divorce. I dreamed of destroying him with my hands, with my mind, utterly destroying him. Wipe-out.

"Then two weeks ago, I woke up one morning, in my room at the clinic, and the hate was gone. I tried to find it again. I counted over all my injuries. It made no difference. The hate was gone, and that frightened me. Can you understand? Hate had been something to hold on to. At least it was a real sensation, it showed I was alive. But now, there was nothing. Just a terrible loneliness, as if I was a place without bounds, stretching for ever. . . ." Margot stopped. "I can't explain."

134

"But my dear, there's no need. The depths of despond are a common enough experience. They have been charted by the saints and by the psychoanalysts, and it's common knowledge that any sensation, even pain, is preferable to total despair. Your own doctor must have explained that to you?"

"I never gave him the chance. I left the clinic. I moved about from place to place, for days. I stayed in hotels. I had the drugs they'd given me at the clinic. I took them, but I seemed to get worse.

"One day I decided to kick them. I took every pill and capsule, except my sleeping-tablets, and poured them down the lavatory. That night I thought I was going mad. I thought of going back to the clinic, but I was convinced that if I did, they'd certify me. In the end I put my bags in the car and just drove. I drove all through the next day, until my petrol ran out. That's how I arrived in Amber. I met your son . . . stayed at The Ram . . . found Bess Tuckett's tombstone."

Margot put her fingers to her forehead and wiped away sweat. "At a moment when I was falling apart, that tombstone kind of pinned me together. Crazy, if you like, but I felt I wanted to know about that woman. She'd been fifty years in her grave, but something in her story pulled me out of my spin and made me feel like a human being again. So I owe her, don't I?"

Gold said gravely. "Yes, perhaps you do." His delicate hand shaded his eyes for a moment, then lifted. "I'm not sure what it is you want of me?"

"Tell me about Ava Campion. Some of the village people swear she was murdered. But Ianthe and Niall Campion, and their friend Randall Jecks, say the story is nonsense. They say Ava died of natural causes."

"That is probably true."

"What did your mother think?"

He frowned. "She seldom spoke of her younger years. She wasn't very happy at Amberside. But I remember that she once mentioned the Tuckett affair, and said that nothing would ever be proved, either way."

XXVII

"So why the suggestion it was murder? How did the idea take such a strong hold?"

"There were some strange circumstances." Mr Gold settled himself more comfortably. "The fact that Bess was always concocting medicines for Ava, that she had a tremendous power over Ava's affections and could persuade her to swallow anything, literally and figuratively. The fact that it was Bess who was the last person to see Ava alive, Bess who helped her to bed. . . ."

"I never knew that."

"Didn't you? I expect Ianthe and Niall decided it was better withheld."

"But I'd have expected Ned Rubidge to know. His mother was Ava's maid. . . ."

"She did not know. She was sent to bed by Ava before the ball was half over. A considerate employer, you see. Perhaps it cost her her life." Gold rubbed a finger along his jaw. "My mother told it this way: On the night of the ball, Amberside was crowded with guests who stayed until dawn. But Ava, who was in poor health, withdrew at about one o'clock. Bess Tuckett went upstairs with her, to help her undress and to give her her medicine . . . a digitalis pill which she took each night upon retiring. She used to wash it down with a small glass of herbal tea, to induce sleep.

"At one thirty Bess returned to the ballroom. She sought out Jerome, who was standing talking with a group of friends. She told him that Ava was 'safely settled', and 'sleeping like the dead'. Certain people were to remember these words.

"At four, Jerome went upstairs himself, and opened the door of his wife's room a little way. He did not go in, not wishing to disturb her, but he listened to her breathing, which was heavy, but not distressed. He saw through the crack of the door that the bedside light was turned low, her little silver handbell in its place on the table beside her, and the overhead bell, which she could use to summon help from the servants, looped as usual to the post at her head. He returned to his guests.

"It was after five when he was finally able to retire, and being very weary, he fell into bed and slept heavily.

"At eleven in the morning, Mrs Rubidge went to rouse her mistress. She found her dead. Ava was lying in the middle of the floor. A light quilt was half under her body, as if she had snatched at it as she staggered from the bed, in her effort to reach the bathroom that connected her room with Jerome's. The overhead bell had been torn loose from its attachment at the ceiling, apparently by repeated jerking. The silver handbell was no longer on the bedside table, where Jerome had seen it.

"It looked, at first glance, as if Ava, in the agony of a severe attack of cardiac asthma, must have knocked the handbell out of reach. Then she dragged so hard at the overhead bell that it broke. Finally she tried to climb out of bed to reach her husband, but collapsed and died before she could do so. The nature of the seizure—its effect on her breathing—would have rendered her unable to call for help.

"There was, as you can imagine, a great deal of coming and going in the room, after the body was found. Doctors,

138

members of the family, servants making the place more seemly.

"There were two doctors staying in the house, and the family doctor was also called in. They had no hesitation in signing the certificate, saying that death was from natural causes. But later, three questions remained unanswered. One, why was the silver bell missing? It was never found. Two, why did Ava suffer the attack on that night in particular, when the attention of the household was elsewhere, and her personal maid out of reach? Three, how did a woman as frail as she was have the strength to pull the cord of the overhead bell from its mooring?

"The story arose that there was some drug other than digitalis in Ava's final glass of herb tea, and that it brought on an asthma attack; that at some point when she was *in extremis*, an unknown person entered her room, removed the handbell, and dragged the cord loose, so that Ava could not summon help.

"That was the story, but it was only a story, and a malicious one, at that. My belief is, it was put about by Edith Rubidge, who was an unbalanced creature, devoted to Ava and jealous of Bess Tuckett."

"Did your mother discuss this with anyone outside the family?"

"My dear, do you imagine she would? It was a scandalous rumour, no more. There was no doubt in the doctors' minds. No post mortem was considered necessary. And what family invites such a thing on the slight pretexts that existed at Amberside? My mother's attitude was 'least said soonest mended'. She only mentioned the subject to me because I showed a morbid curiosity about it. She said that Bess Tuckett, if she had been guilty of murder, was now dead and buried, so justice was achieved, if a little belatedly."

139

Mr Gold rose to his feet. "And now, would you like to see the portraits?"

He led Margot up one flight of the spiral stairway to a gallery overlooking the living-room, and there indicated a group of pictures at the far end.

"These will interest you most. They are the dramatis personae of the play."

The portraits were carefully arranged and lighted. Margot moved from one to another. Jerome's father, mother and sister. Jerome himself, first as a young man and again in the year of his death. Passion, arrogance, eagerness had been tempered by the years, but not subdued. Not an easy man to live with, but not dull. Next to him was his wife; a small face with a broad forehead, a thin little neck, a smile both sweet and enigmatic. Beyond her, a portrait of her son Dicky. Technically less good than the others, the painting showed the Campion features—Chilli had them, she now realised—but not the Campion fire. Next to affable Dicky, his wife Ianthe, as a young woman. She had indeed been beautiful, with all the attributes of line and colour. She looked, also, rather stupid, but that might have been the artist's fault. Margot turned to Mr Gold.

"What about Bess? Have you one of her?"

"Nothing official. But my mother was good at sketching, and made a drawing of her. Strangely enough, it was only about ten days before she was drowned. Here it is, along here. . . .

The sketch hung alone . . . symbolically, Margot thought . . . and although it was amateur work, it had immediacy and vigour.

Bess Tuckett had been too tall and heavy-boned for beauty. Had she lived, she might have become a strapping Wagnerian prima donna, but in her late teens she had had a magnificence of the flesh.

The drawing showed her seated on a stone bench, with

140

behind her the suggestion of an autumnal garden, and a great house. Amberside, clearly. Beside her on the bench was a jumble of articles; a box of artist's colours, jars, brushes, a gauze scarf. In her lap was a lute. Her head was raised, as if she had been absorbed in her music and had been interrupted. Her hair, thick and curling, hung loose about her shoulders and she smiled directly into the eyes of the viewer, bold, frank and welcoming.

Margot stared at the picture for a long time. Something about the lute struck her as familiar, and she moved in closer to study the detail. There was a decoration round the throat of the instrument, a minute chain of flowers. Campions.

As comprehension began to flood in upon her, she stepped back and turned to Mr Gold.

"That lute is in the Barn Museum. It's Jerome's."

"Is it? I've never studied the holy relics, I'm afraid. I suppose it's silly, but my mother didn't see eye to eye with Ianthe, and after Dicky was killed, she never went to Amber. I've only visited it a few times, on business matters."

Margot glanced back at the sketch of Bess. "Whatever her faults," she said, "that woman was never a fool. If Jerome was guilty of murder, then she would have known it."

"Jerome guilty?" Gold was shocked out of his calm.

"Well, isn't it a reasonable supposition? He had the same motive as Bess for wishing his wife dead, and far more opportunity to poison her."

"Really, my dear Mrs Wootten . . ."

"Isn't that the reason," said Margot inexorably, "that your family avoided all talk about Ava's death? They suspected murder, and thought that Jerome could be accused?"

"Nonsense!"

141

"But it's a fact that they hushed up certain suspicious matters! You've admitted as much. And later, when the rumours started, they didn't try to squash them. They allowed the guilt to rest on Bess, even after she was dead. It saved them embarrassment!"

"You mustn't get so excited. You're talking rubbish."

Margot gave an exclamation of impatience and began to hurry along the gallery. Mr Gold rushed after her.

"Where are you going?"

"Back to Amber."

"You mustn't. It might be dangerous for you."

She paused at the head of the stair. "Might it? Why?"

He shook his head angrily. "I shall come with you."

"No thank you. If you're there, nothing will happen."

"That is precisely ... wait, please ... I do beg of you to consider ... I wish I had never spoken. ..."

Down the stairs they went, and out into the street, Mr Gold still protesting. As Margot climbed into the Fiat, he said sharply, "I shall inform the police, you know."

She smiled at him. "Of what? No crime has been committed, you told me."

"I shall inform them, Dr Wootten, of your whereabouts."

The car door slammed. The car swung out into the traffic. Mr Gold, having watched it vanish eastwards, hastened back into the house and put through a call to Amber. After a brief delay, a woman's voice answered.

"The Ram."

"Nancy, it's John Gold. Is Chilli there?"

"He went over to Kersey, Mr Gold. Said he wouldn't be late, though. Shall I ask him to phone you back?"

"Please. Tell him it's urgent."

"Surely. Is there anything I can do for you?"

"I don't think ... but yes, perhaps you could speak to Will Asher. Tell him that Mrs Margot Wootten is on her

142

way back to Amber. Tell him she is talking very wildly, and I think that he or Chilli must look out for her."

"I'll tell 'im. And when Chilli comes in, you'll be at home, will you?"

"Yes, I'll wait here."

Nancy Rubidge replaced the receiver. The man beside her said, "What was that?"

"John Gold, to say the woman's coming back. I'm to warn Will Asher."

She left the inn, heading for the garage.

The man watched from the front window until he saw her vanish into the workshop. Then he went quietly through to the gun-room at the back of the building; collected what he needed, and took the path that led to the river.

XXVIII

FOR THE SECOND time, the Fiat negotiated Cobbledick Hill. From its summit, Amber showed as scattered
lights under scattered stars. It was a cold clear night,
without wind.

Margot drove down towards the village, past the fields
of Tuckett's Farm and the dark hulk of Amberside. She
had entered the belt of woods along the river when the
shots came.

She heard the bullets fly over the car's bonnet, and the
report multiply by echo among the trees. Without pausing
to think, she thrust her foot down on the accelerator. The
Fiat lurched forward, skidding round the curve. A hundred
yards ahead lay the fork in the road. Right, over the
bridge, lay the village, left, up the hill, the Dower House.
She slowed her pace.

Behind her now was absolute silence. On which side was
the gunman? The safest course would be to drive into
Amber and report to the police. She half turned towards
the bridge, but at the last moment, pulled on the wheel
and took the left-hand fork. The Fiat climbed. The woods
closed in. She drove as fast as she dared, expecting every
minute to hear the crash of bullets. Nothing happened.
She reached the clearing on the brow of the hill.

The Dover House was in darkness but lights glowed in

the barn. Parked in a corner of the yard was Niall Campion's Lamborghini, and next to it a Rover saloon. Margot put the Fiat into the line and walked to the nearest door. She rang the bell, but there was no response. Putting out a hand, she tried the latch. The door gave. She stepped into the corridor, where a single lamp burned; closed the door gently and quietly and walked along to the barn.

They were there, all three of them. Ianthe Campion and Randall Jecks sat like two stiff old puppets in the easy chairs at the near end. A trolley bearing decanters and glasses had been wheeled close to the reading table. At the window stood Niall, one hand still grasping a fold of the curtain. He let it fall as Margot entered the room.

"Dr Wootten." He approached her with a hesitant step. He seemed both nervous and puzzled. "That must have been a poacher in the woods. I'm afraid we don't run to keepers any more. I hope he didn't scare you?"

"He most certainly did."

"I'm so sorry. Would you like a drink?"

"No thanks." She stopped directly in front of him. "It seems you were expecting me, Mr Campion."

"Oh . . . well, yes. In a way." He shifted back a pace or two. "A queer thing. Nancy Rubidge called me on the phone and said you were coming to Amber. She was very anxious . . . about you."

"There's no need. I simply want to talk." Margot glanced at the man and woman behind her. "To all of you."

"Of course. Please sit down." Niall indicated a chair. "Did you by any chance catch sight of this . . . ah . . . sharpshooter?"

"I didn't see him. I know who it was."

"You do? In that case, shouldn't one phone the police?"

"You can, if you like. I don't propose to, yet." Margot settled herself, glancing about the shadowy barn. Only the lights at this end were lit. They shone on the table where the Campion lute lay.

"It was Ned Rubidge who fired the shots," she said. "Do you want to know why?"

Silence. Then Niall spoke with sudden irritation. "I would certainly like some explanation of this whole extraordinary week. Since it all started with your intrusions, Dr Wootten. . . ."

"It didn't start with me, it won't end with me. It's your story more than mine. But I'll tell you how I became part of it. It was when I saw the tombstone on Bess Tuckett's grave. An urn filled with poisonous plants. That was the first question: who set up the stone, and why?"

Nobody spoke. Randall Jecks was fiddling with his empty glass, and Ianthe Campion had fallen into the pose that seemed characteristic of her, eyes closed, wrists limp.

"I spoke to Coker Brown and Zillah," said Margot, "and they were interested enough to do some checking. They couldn't discover who ordered the stone.

"The other part of the question—why it was erected—was answered for me by Ned Rubidge. He told me Bess Tuckett was a poisoner. She poisoned Ava Campion on the night of the Amberside Ball. Her motive was to marry her lover, Jerome Campion, and get her hands on his worldly goods, which were many."

Niall made a gesture of annoyance. "If you mean to revive that old slander. . . ."

"Revive? That's not the right word, Mr Campion. There's a very strange angle to all this, and that is that there was no public scandal about Ava's death. Nothing in the national papers, no inquest, certainly no hint of a *cause célèbre*, despite the fact that the Campion family was widely known, even famous. That such a tale never leaked beyond the limits of Amber can mean only one thing—that not a single soul spoke of it outside this village. There must have been a conspiracy of silence that bound every man, woman and child. And that is an amazing feat."

"We were agreed," said Randall Jecks, "upon the need to preserve the decencies."

"You weren't agreed at all," retorted Margot. "The village people were certain Bess Tuckett was a murderess. Your circle was sure Ava died a natural death. Silence suited you all. Why? That was my second question."

"Then I can only say," snapped Randall, "that if your other questions are as foolish as the first two, then it is a waste of time to listen to you."

Margot looked at him. "The third question concerns you, Mr Jecks, and it arose on Friday night, when I attended that choir practice." She glanced at Niall, who had returned to the window and was standing with his back to them. "There was a silly argument, you remember, because Chilli Gold, Will Asher and Ned Rubidge had conspired to sing the Campion songs to lute accompaniment. It was a trivial plan, yet you, Mr Jecks, blew your top. You stormed out of the church in a tantrum, and you lost no time in reporting the squabble to Mr Campion, who in turn put pressure on Will Asher."

Niall swung round. "You mean Asher told you . . . ?"

"No. I was in the workshop when you quarrelled with him, I heard what you said, and I couldn't help wondering why you were swatting a fly with a sledgehammer."

"Asher infuriates me, he's been a thorn in my flesh for years. He deliberately inflames village feelings against me and my business enterprises."

"That still doesn't explain why you felt you must rush to defend Mr Jecks. But let that pass. My third question is this: why did Mr Jecks so violently resent the Campion

147

songs being set to lute accompaniment? Having heard them sung that way, I'm dead sure it's the best way, and any musician would say the same. So why all the fuss? It puzzled me for some time, until I arrived at a simple answer. The Campion songs were originally written for lute accompaniment. If Jecks denies this, he does so for a good reason, namely, that he is not the composer of the songs. He has passed himself off as the composer, when all he in fact did was arrange the work and get it published in his own name."

"Outrageous!" Jecks was on his feet and dancing like a courting crane. "That is a libellous statement!"

"It's a statement about a criminal and despicable action," said Margot. "Or do you imagine that stealing a creative work is less important than stealing a material object?"

"You have not an atom of proof for this abominable suggestion."

"I didn't come here to discuss proof. I came to get at the truth, and the truth is that you couldn't in all your born days have composed anything as good as the Campion Cycle. You haven't the talent. It was composed by Bess Tuckett, and the words were written by Jerome Campion after the composition of the music, not before. When Jerome showed you those poems at Amberside, the music was already written.

"If you look at the form of the poems, you can tell at once, by their shape, that they were never meant to be read as pure poetry. The balance is wrong, the emphasis and scansion is wrong. But set them against a melody that carries some words and shades others, and you can see the true effect. The Campion Cycle is music to which words have been set . . . not the other way about.

"And it's true, isn't it, Mr Jecks, that Bess Tuckett was intending to give the first public performance of her songs

148

at the concert Jerome arranged for her—the one held on the night she died? Those were the anonymous songs listed in the programme. It was their presentation that so inflamed the village people, that they broke up the concert?

"After Bess and Jerome were dead, you saw your way clear to an easy reputation. You stole the work, and put your name to it. Because the lute was Bess Tuckett's instrument, and you feared people might recognise her authorship, you scored the music not for lute, but for piano, flute and recorder. It took a born musician like Chilli Gold to sense the deception, and correct it."

"A pack of lies! Do you imagine my reputation—and it is not inconsiderable—can be challenged by such hysterical accusations?"

"Very likely, yes. Many people have wondered how you ever managed to write such music. You're known as a 'one-shot' artist, a failed composer who never repeated his first, solitary success. Your reputation, among the *cognoscenti*, hangs by one thread, and you're well aware of it. To preserve that one miserable claim to fame, you have connived at a number of things; the destruction of the countryside, the smearing of Bess Tuckett's name, even the fact of murder. . . ."

"A moment!"

Niall Campion's voice sounded shrill, as he signalled to Jecks to be quiet. Jecks subsided unwillingly in his chair and Niall stepped forward, watching Margot with bright and wary eyes.

"You are being very foolish, Dr Wootten."

"I don't think so."

"Indeed you are. Making libellous statements before witnesses. If we excuse you, it is simply because we know that you are, temporarily, of unsound mind. . . ."

"I'm perfectly sane."

"I question that. After your first visit here, I took the

149

precaution of making some enquiries of my own. I'm not without resources. I learned that you have been in a mental hospital, until very recently."

"I was in the Lovell Clinic. It is not a mental home, it's a clinic for the treatment of neurodiseases. I had typhus fever."

"According to my informant, you suffered from hallucinations."

"That's a symptom of typhus in the acute stage. It passes, quite quickly, as mine did. I was left with problems of insomnia and depression, and that was why I went into hospital—as a voluntary patient."

"You left before the doctors recommended you to do so."

"So I did." Margot grinned at him. "Before you make any further threats, Mr Campion, let me say that I know I have no case in law against Mr Jecks. I simply want to let him know that I know it was Bess Tuckett who wrote the Campion songs. Nothing more."

"Nothing more?" Jecks was stammering with fury. "You call that nothing? To accuse me of piracy, of plagiarism? Why, Mrs Campion herself will testify for me. She will tell you that Jerome read us his poems, and that she herself invited me, after his death, to set them to music. As a tribute, you hear, a tribute to his memory! Oh, this is all too disgusting! Ianthe, isn't it true, what I say? You invited me?"

"I did." The old woman faced Margot with weary indifference. "Of course I did, Randall. Don't worry about this poor creature. She is deluded."

"You did not invite Mr Jecks to arrange the songs. The music was never in your hands. It belonged to Bess, and she would never have shown it to you, tone deaf as you are. She despised and mistrusted you, Mrs Campion. But

150

Mr Jecks was convenor of the arrangements for that last concert. He must have seen the score."

Ianthe shrugged. "It's really very stupid of you to invent all these tales. No one will believe them. Why should Randall tell lies, why should I tell lies?"

Margot stared at her in silence for a moment. Then she said, "Everyone lied. You, your family, Mr Jecks, the whole village. That answers the second question I put tonight. You were all involved in a conspiracy to conceal the fact of murder."

Outside the barn, a dog began to bark. They heard footsteps approaching at a run, and fists pounding at the window. Niall Campion went over and pulled aside the curtain.

Three men stood in the courtyard, Chilli Gold, Will Asher, and Coker Brown.

"Open up!"

As Niall fumbled with the sash, Chilli caught the lower frame and flung it up, swung himself headlong into the room.

"Where's Ned? The old bugger's loose with a gun. . . ."

"You stand still, lad. You stay there." The voice came from the main door of the barn.

Framed against the darkness like some backwoods prophet, wild hair glinting and eyes a-stare, rifle cradled in the crook of his arm, was Ned Rubidge.

XXIX

"I TOLD YOU!" He took a stride into the room. and the gun pointed now at Margot. "I told you, let the dead rest. No call to wake the past, 'at's best forgotten."

Niall Campion walked forward.

"Ned, there's a good fellow, give me the gun."

Rubidge's great arm reached out and brushed Niall aside like thistledown.

"I'm talkin' to the missus. You get out of Amber, lady Go back where you came from and leave us alone."

"I can't, Mr Rubidge. She won't rest, you know that."

"Rest? What rest did she earn, with murder on 'er soul?"

"Bess Tuckett did not commit murder."

"I told you . . ."

". . . and I am telling you, Bess Tuckett committed no crime. But there was murder done, and three of you in this room tonight saw it done. You witnessed the murder of Jerome Campion and Bess Tuckett."

Randall Jecks made a small moaning sound. As Margot looked at him he muttered, "They drowned. They drowned. The post mortem showed water in their lungs."

"But their bodies bore multiple injuries."

"What do you expect? They were battered as they were carried downstream. The river was in flood. . . ."

"They were battered by stones taken from the river's edge. They ran together from the Wool Hall, and the villagers who had been pelting them with garbage, followed them to the tow-path and pelted them with rocks. Perhaps it was only Bess they wanted to kill. Perhaps Jerome tried to shield her, and was stoned. Perhaps they tried to cross the ford, to escape, and were swept away." She turned to the old man. "Who cast the first stone, Ned? Was it you?"

"No!" He was shouting, his face pallid. "I never. I ran, I ran away, I couldn't watch. . . ."

"And you," Margot moved towards Randall Jecks. "You were a witness. You were ill on the night of the concert, and stayed at home. Your upper windows overlook the river. You must have heard the noise of that rabble, running down to the tow-path. A mob howling, there's no sound on earth you can confuse with that. You saw a lynching, and you kept your mouth shut because you knew too much of the truth to want to be involved. Isn't that right? You kept quiet, and in due course you were rewarded by the patronage of the Campion family, and the servility of the people of Amber."

This time Jecks did not protest, but gazed at Margot with the hard, bright eyes of fear.

"I've wondered," she said, "why there was no police enquiry. I suppose that by the time the village policeman was called, it was all over. A drowning fatality, with two most reliable witnesses to tell how it happened. Mr Jecks, watching from his window in Ringan's Close. Ianthe Campion, watching from her window at Amberside. You saw it all, didn't you, Mrs Campion?"

The old woman did not raise her head. "I saw them drown."

"You saw them stoned. You stood at the window of the master bedroom, and watched the whole thing, and you were glad, because with them out of the way, there was no one between you and the possessions you were so greedy to own."

Mrs Campion seemed to consider. "I was glad about the woman's death," she said at last. "She was immoral, and a murderess."

Ned Rubidge shouted, "Yes! 'At's true. She killed Mrs Ava, we know that."

"So your mother told you, Ned, and you believed her, being only sixteen years old at the time. But have you ever thought who told your mother?"

His lips, thick and blotched, thrust out and in. "We knew. Poison, she used. Everyone knew."

"But who told everyone?" Margot shifted closer to the old man, speaking softly. "Who spread the stories about Bess, who invented lies about the night Ava Campion died, and kept on spreading those lies? They were lies, you know. Nobody gave Ava poison. She died of natural causes."

"My mother told me!"

"Your mother repeated what she had been told, and it was lies. Shall I tell you the truth? Listen. On the night of the Christmas Ball at Amberside, Ava was not well. She should not have attended it, but felt it was her duty. She acted as hostess and moved among her guests. About midnight, she sent your mother away, telling her not to wait up any longer. At one, she felt too ill to remain at the ball, so she asked Bess Tuckett to take her upstairs. Bess did so, helped Ava to undress, gave her her pill and her sleeping-draught, and waited with her till she fell asleep. Then Bess returned to the party.

"At four o'clock, Jerome went up to see his wife, but did not enter her room. He stopped at the door, heard her breathing evenly, saw that her silver bell was in place beside her, and the overhead bell intact. He left her to sleep.

154

"Shortly after that visit, Ava Campion suffered a fatal heart attack. Perhaps, as the seizure began, she cried out, rang her bell. The house was full of the noise of the ball, and all the servants busy. No one came to her from downstairs. But I think one person heard her, and came to her door. Stood there, perhaps, listening as Ava tried to reach the bathroom. Heard her collapse and die. That person was a ruthless person, and greedy, and stupid except where her own gain was concerned. She saw a way to profit by the situation, with no danger to herself. She saw that if the suspicion arose that Ava's death was not natural, but had been hastened by malice, then the obvious suspects would be Bess Tuckett and Jerome. And if they were suspect, then they could not marry, and there would be no fresh rivals for Amberside and the Campion money.

"So this person walked quietly into the bedroom where Ava lay dead. She picked up the little silver handbell and slipped it into a pocket or purse. She reached up—she was a tall, strong girl—and dragged at the overhead bell so sharply that it came away from its fastenings. And then she walked quickly downstairs and helped to speed the parting guests.

"If any servant answered that final peal of the bell, then it would be to find Ava Campion dead—in suspicious circumstances. If no one came, well . . . sooner or later she must be found. Unfortunately, when the discovery was made next morning, things didn't go according to plan. Doctors, servants, and the Campion family—with one exception—were anxious to smooth things over. There was no hint of murder, the death certificate was signed and Ava Campion was buried decently without any unpleasant talk.

"Still, there was time for that later, plenty of time to stir up gossip, using the weapons to hand. The weapons were people, Bess Tuckett who was brash and arrogant

155

and made enemies, Randall Jecks who would say anything to oblige a patron, and your own mother, who was jealous and unhappy and already in the grip of religious mania.

"Ask yourself, Mr Rubidge, who can have put the thought of murder into your mother's mind? Who was close enough to work on her every day, to convince her that Bess was a wicked and sinful woman who must be punished?"

"I . . . don't . . . know. . . ."

"But you do know. It was Mrs Campion who stood to gain most when Bess and Jerome died. And it was Mrs Campion who incited the people of Amber to the point when they committed a lynching."

The people in the room had edged closer together. Chilli Gold had shifted towards Margot, Niall stood with a hand on Jecks's shoulder. Only Ianthe Campion seemed perfectly at ease. She roused herself from what might have been an after-dinner reverie.

"It is all nonsense, Ned. The girl is insane. What she says has no more weight than moonshine. Give Niall the gun, and sit down like a sensible man."

Her son took an obedient step towards Rubidge, but the old man shook his head in warning. "You be still." He returned his gaze to Margot.

"How do I know you told the truth?"

"Did I tell the truth of what happened at the river?"

He shook his head slowly. "How can I tell? I ran away. My mother never spoke of that night to me. No one spoke of it. The people went away, they left Amber . . . ." A thought seemed to strike him and he shuffled across to tower over Jecks's chair.

"You saw what happened. Was it like she said?"

"No. They drowned."

"On God's oath, you swear it?"

156

"Yes."

Rubidge fingered the stock of the gun. "All right then, will you swear something else? Will you swear that Mrs Campion spread no word against Bess Tuckett and Jerome Campion?"

"She said nothing against them."

"Nor wish them dead?"

"No."

"Your oath on it?"

"Yes."

"Ask him," said Margot suddenly, "ask him to swear on the Campion lute."

"What?" Ned Rubidge jerked up his chin. Margot brushed past him and went to the little table where the lute lay, picked it up and brought it back.

"This afternoon," she said, "Mr John Gold showed me a sketch of Bess Tuckett. It was done ten days before she died. It showed her at Amberside. She had this lute on her lap, and on the bench beside her were paint pots and a length of gauze."

She turned the lute over, "It's been mended, you see? Here's the join, in the belly. Jerome would have had it mended in Amber, and the best at the craft was Bess Tuckett. If she mended the lute, she would follow local custom, wouldn't she? She would cut out the damaged wood and replace it, matching the varnish very closely. She would strap the inside of the lute with strips of gauze, and she would sign the strapping; once with the Campions' own mark, and once with a few notes of appropriate music. Mr Jecks, I don't go much for Bible oaths, but will you swear on this lute that you are the composer of the Campion songs?"

Jecks said nothing. His eyes were fixed on the lute. Ned Rubidge bent forward.

"Well, man? You were ready enough with words, before."

"This is nonsense. You will prove nothing."

"Did you write 'em, or not?"

"Of course I wrote them."

Margot ran her fingers along the smooth neck of the lute. She wondered briefly how old it was and how much music it had made before it was silenced. Then she raised it level with her shoulder and brought it down sharply on the arm of Jecks's chair.

The wood cracked and sprang apart like a boat too long ashore. A section fell right out, and she picked it up quickly, handing it to Ned Rubidge.

The old man stared at it for some moments. Then he looked at Jecks.

"You bloody thief."

The strip of gauze had been signed twice; once with a campion flower, and once with the opening notes of the Campion Cycle.

XXX

"SHE NEVER TURNED a hair," said Chilli in disbelief. "You never even got near her. Sitting there in her chair as if she was watching some boring old movie. . . ." He looked at Coker. "What do you think she'll do?"

"Nothing. She knows she is safe. She is guilty of falsifying evidence, of incitement to murder, but it's all long past. It will never be brought home to her this side of death."

"She has to be insane."

"No. She is a cold, greedy and rather dull woman who has got away with a most dreadful crime. She'll go on living at the Dower House. She'll come to church, most likely. Do you realise that all these years she's been taking communion? Her donations have helped to pay my salary. I must tell you I'm far more exercised about what is my own course of action, than what will be Ianthe's."

"You will pray for her soul," said Zillah shortly. She was making coffee for them. Her husband and Chilli were perched on the kitchen fender, Margot sprawled, nearly asleep, in the rocking chair. Now she opened her eyes.

"I'm sorry. I never meant to shift a burden on to you."

"But of course you didn't. Zillah's quite right. It's a good thing I know the truth of it."

Chilli was still angry. "And that bastard Jecks. We'll

never prove he stole those songs. A stanza in the lute, a few notes that anyone could whistle. Jecks has only to say she picked it up from him, and we'd be thrown out of court."

Margot shook her head. "The point is that Bess did write them, and knew she'd written them. That's all that matters in the long run."

When they had talked the events of the night to a standstill, Chilli and Margot set out for the inn.

As they passed the wicket gate of St Ringan's, they turned through it by common consent, and walked to the far corner of the graveyard.

They found the grass there much trampled. The tombstone on Bess Tuckett's grave had been overset, and rolled into the ditch. The impact had cracked it clean across.

"Ned and Will," said Chilli, and Margot nodded.

They made their way back to the main road. The village, which Margot had first seen shrouded in mist, now floated clear on the full tide of the moon. She put out her hand and felt Chilli's fingers lace through hers with a firm grip as he turned his head to smile at her.